"WORMS IN THE NEEDLE"

By

JONATHAN MOON

And

Brought to you with loving trepidation from

Welcome To Morbidbooks. Where Everything Bleeds.

(click on any image in this book for hyperlink)

Morbidbooks Is A Grotesque Bizarro Ballet Where The Most Profane Things Occur. An Impious And Perverse Dwelling Of Dark Revulsion. A Cozy Cottage Where Torture Porn And Brutal Bible Tales Are Devised. A Quiet Place To Relax And Spin Tales Of Depravity And Wickedness. A Halfway House For The Disturbed Where Rules No Longer Apply. A Safe Haven For Deviant Serial Killers To Hatch Their Wretched Schemes. Bring Your Pets. The Tasty Ones Are Always Welcome.

https://www.morbidbooks.wordpress.com

MAN·IS·BVT·A·WORM

Punch cartoon by Linley Sambourne, 1882.

Romance at the end of the world is simply not dying alone. -
Wormer

CHAPTER ONE

THE PARTY IS OVER.

I can tell because things become hellishly plain as reality returns. The neon flowers wilt and the shimmering flesh peels off the surrounding angels. Once it flakes away, the angels collapse into puddles of hissing goop and withered petals blow into them, hurried along by unseen winds. My spit looses its sweet taste to the black flavor of ash. The glowing birds in the bright orange sky burst into small sparkly novas. The sky itself weeps and tears, streaking down like a ruined painting as the dismal gray of life wheezes back before my eyes. I don't blink; praying silently for one last desperate taste of the high.

Lila feels it too. She writhes on the mattress next to me, moans of ecstasy warping into groans. She rolls into the fetal position as her stomach cramps at the fleeing high. I notice the stains beneath her, ambiguous streaks of white and puddles of flaking brown, and see the abstract shapes of unnamable monsters and the atrocities they eternally commit. I stare at her back and count her ribs. When I reach out and rub my finger up along them, she uncurls and rolls towards me. Her eyes are open and glazed, as I'm sure mine are. Her eyes aren't as bright as they used to be. She stares at me for a few minutes before she sees me. I stare back not bothering to hide my fuming jealousy.

That's the last time she gets the bigger worm.

Tears form in her eyes and I can almost feel the lump in her throat. It's gone and she wants to cry. I'd rather chase down more Worms than cry about it but everybody reacts to the Worms differently. I slip away to my own neon colored utopia where things with wings fan me and comfort me when the living neon worm dissolves under my skin. Lila told me once they wrap around her like a giant fuzzy neon hug. I imagine her high shedding off her like snake skin and flaking to the filthy floor next to the mattress. I slap her boney rump and stand up.

Once on my feet, I sway in place a few times. I look around the room for my clothes and see them scattered amongst the debris of broken ceiling tile, crushed half bricks, and shattered glass. My bare feet care not the terrain between them and another needle full of worm. Shards of glass multiply under my weight as I gather my wardrobe. I pull on my pants and my shirt while Lila stares at me with her pools of misery. I don't see either of my sandals and I leave bloody foot prints in my wake as I walk back to the mattress. She wants me to hold her but my arms and my love don't feel like her high. It will only make us both angry, eventually, but I lay down next to her anyways. She crawls into my arms and nuzzles her head under my chin. Her breath stutters and her body twitches. I run my fingers through her tar black hair while counting the cracks in the ceiling.

"I'm crashing," she whispers, "like, bad, this time."

"It's bad every time. That's why we do more."

She slaps my hand away from her hair as she rolls onto my chest to face me.

"Oh, you aren't crashing? I'm the only one of us strung the fuck out?"

I don't want to argue with a comedown.

"My guts feel like they've sprouted bleeding thorns!" I scream in her face. "Get your clothes on and let's go find us Billy Shanks."

"And it we can't find Billy Shanks?" Her crash whines at me.

"Then we'll find a different Digger. We're getting some Worms tonight."

Lila smiles at the word but without the worm dissolving under her skin it seems empty. She kisses my sweaty forehead with freezing lips and climbs out of bed. I watch the muscles in her calves when she walks to her pile of clothes. She bends over to rifle through them and I stare at her sex. Soft, pink and hiding in thick, black pubic hair. Before I can get aroused, the color drains from her skin till she looks like a granite statue. She picks a bright green shirt up from the floor and over her head. Once she pulls it snug so her pert nipples poke out like puppy dog noses it becomes a faded white. Her smile fades when she sees my scowl. I don't know what to say so I just get up and find my missing sandals. Blood sticks them to my feet.

"Don't be mad." She tells me as she pulls up her patchwork pants. I know each patch is a different color but I'm seeing each as an identical fuzzy gray. She smiles her freezing lips at me and her alabaster white hair falls over her left eye.

"I'm not," I tell her as I walk through the door-less doorway into the hallway, "just hurry up."

She catches up just a few doors down and grabs my hand with hers.

"Slow down." She whisper/scowls while peeking into other door-less rooms in the abandoned motel hallway. Her crash only enhances her paranoia. She squeezes my hand when she sees other people in the rooms. I pay them no mind; too driven in my need to bother watching someone else feel how I should feel. We pass a doorway emitting the sound of two men deep in the arms of worm induced euphoria punctuated with loud rhythmic banging sounds that drops moldy flecks of paint from the ceiling. We walk through the paint deluge and down the stair well.

The walls are covered with graffiti; curse words and dozens of crude drawing of Worms. The floors are littered with garbage and human waste. The once elegant red and gold carpet has streaks of ominous crimson and patches of scorch marks on nearly every floor. A wet bloody hand print smears the faded white walls as if someone bled their way down the stairs only moments before us. We reach the ground floor and step over the corpse sprawled across the bottom two stairs.

"Goodbye, Bob." I tell the swollen body with the word 'Bob' carved across his ample belly.

"Look," Lila points at Bob's feet, "someone has finally stolen his shoes."

Sure enough, swollen green toes with black toenails point back up the stairway.

"Dead toes for up, bloody hand prints for down," I answer.

Lila hugs me close and tells me, "You're a poet, baby."

We walk fully embracing each other like a drunken four legged crab through the lobby. Two more corpses float in the stagnant water of the fountain, bobbing and rolling from the motion of the pump. A bubbling froth of filthy bubbles mask the corpse with the bell hop uniform upturned face. The three metal cherubs spitting foul piss colored water are all draped in pastel colored feather boas. If I was high on worm, the boas would be glowing and the fat little cherubs would be whispering me seductive lullabies.

As we near the ruins of the reception area we hear soft sobbing sounds. We untangle from each other because sadness strikes us deeper, affects us in far darker ways, when we are crashing. I reach down and silently remove my flip-flops but the woman ducked behind the burnt out front desk hears our foot falls anyways. Sad feet are heavy feet and we couldn't help but clomp on the blood streaked marble floor. The woman jumps up from her hiding spot, trips over the charred counter, and stumbles towards us. We do a very inconsiderate ballet in order to avoid catching her. She tumbles past us and face plants onto the blood slick floor. We do our best to act as if we still don't see or hear her as her sobs turn to confused shrieks of rage.

"What is your problem? What is going on here? What happened to the city?"

Her questions are so outdated and ridiculous our worm craving wanes momentarily so we can laugh at her. She doesn't respond well. Her rage loses out to her confusion and her screaming turns to wailing. We laugh even harder which only serves to make her cry even louder. We near the doors and she remains frozen in place by the reception desk wailing away too scared to try conversing with us further. A shirtless man, rail thin from worm addiction, dives out of the shadows next to the elevators screaming, "Shut up! Shut up! Shut up!" He is holding both hands over his ears to block the horrid noise of sorrow and since each hand is clutching a large kitchen knife he looks like he has long sharp metal bunny ears.

The woman turns her wailing at him and he responds by burying one knife in her gut and the other into her wide open mouth. Her wail gags into wet gurgling sounds. He twists the knife in her gut and wiggles the one in her mouth while still spitting, "Shut up! Shut up! Shut up!" Once her twitching corpse obeys his command, he removes both blades in gory unison. Her body slumps to the floor in the growing puddle of her blood. The man regards us briefly but dismisses us as crashing and harmless. He reaches down, grabs the corpse by the foot, and drags it back to the shadows by the elevators leaving a splotchy crimson trail which criss-crosses older, eerily similar dragging stains.

It is almost impossible to tell that this was one of the nicest hotels in the city only a few short weeks ago.

CHAPTER TWO

THE SKY ISN'T ALWAYS BLUE ANY MORE.

When the rolling black clouds allow peeks within them, we can catch fleeting glimpses of the bright red sky smeared across the fading blue, huge sky-born bruises. Seeing the angry stratosphere still sends a shock to the small piece of mind that remembers the peaceful blue before the Worms. That part of my brain forgets more and more, and cares less and less. Lila stares at the sky, eyes wide taking in the terror-scape above us. Apparently, her brain still cares.

"Why is the sky red again?" She asks suddenly shielding her eyes as if the black clouds inflict the same blinding glare as the sun.

I clear my dry throat, wincing as my breath slices the tender flesh, and tell her, "The sky is red because everything is linked. The people bleed, the rivers bleed, and so the sky bleeds."

The end of the world snuck up on everyone. It didn't erupt with a bang and leave the buildings and trees in ashes. It wasn't a virus that raised the dead. It was the Worms; glowing Worms they found deep in an Australian desert. A team of archeologists stumbled into an ancient tomb and brought crates full of the twisting, shimmering things to the surface. The world marveled over the bizarre new species and their fantastic phosphorous glow. First they were news (from weird news of the week to head-lines the world over), then pop culture (from clever tee shirts to nauseatingly adorable internet memes to energy drinks), next the newest designer drug (with a high that rendered all others ridiculously tame and unsatisfying), and finally the curse that decimated mankind (sweet glowing demise).

Men of science were the first ones to inject them. A sanitized laboratory was the first place humans experienced the euphoric effects of the living worm dissolving under their skin. I can't imagine the colors they saw in the stainless steel and bleach white around them. How men of logic decided to squish living creatures into needles and then themselves is a mystery that not even Robert Stack could help solve but I'd be willing to bet it was those damned colors. A group of such scientists formed the first of many Worm-worshipping cults and praised the benefits of main-lining the bright Worms. They cast aside their conventional teachings in favor of the glowing warm high and proclaimed themselves The Church of the Dying Star.

Others followed quickly but The Church of the Dying Star was the first and is now one last organizations of any kind still functioning. They were the first to discover and preach gospel of the Worms. They were the first to realize the Worms grew in graveyard dirt best, the older the graveyard the better the creatures seemed to flourish.

Its members are credited with spreading the Worms to the Americas and Europe. Then, Asia and Africa after that. People were addicted before the first time they juiced up. Being anywhere in a ten foot radius of a living worm stirred something within us simple weak humans; a primal need that dwarfed our natural instincts. Very, very few can resist the call of the worm. And they were left to deal with everything when it went to shit.

A twelve percent unemployment rate is nothing compared to ninety-three percent of the world just not doing their jobs. No people to open and run the stores and gas stations. No security to protect the businesses from dangerous unstable looters. No media to report and distribute word of other countries falling to themselves. No congress men and women to turn the wheels of government. No police to stop the nightly gang rapes and innumerable murders. No pilots to fly the planes to evacuate survivors. Chaos swept the world as its people lost themselves to the twisted paradise the Worms give.

"You're a poet, baby," Lila coos at me, stirring me from my memories.

"I'm not a poet," I tell her slackly, "I'm a fucking junkie just looking to get high."

Her eyes sparkle empty and deep but she doesn't give the hurt a voice. I can respect her for that. I tilt my head and half shrug my shoulders; an awkward attempt at less an apology than letting her know not to take it personal. She turns away without returning my nod. She takes a few angry steps when something falls from above and lands brutally on the side walk in front of us.

CHAPTER THREE

THE BODY EXPLODES ON THE CONCRETE LIKE A FLESH-BOMB.

It lands back-first forcing broken ribs though the tender flesh of chest and stomach. Organs fling forth like confetti from a party popper. Intestines erupt as a ball but unravel in mid-air like a morbid magic trick. A balloon of blood shoots up from the impact, pops, and rains back down on the corpse. The blood forms a perfect circle around the body the same color as the swirling sky above.

Lila gasps and shudders. She turns back to me, her face painted in crimson streaks and her hair plastered to her cheeks with gore. I can't suppress my laughter.

Her anger glows neon in her eyes, the homicidal shimmer all Worm users share, and I turn away to look above me for where the body could have fallen from. I still feel her glare like glowing hate-daggers jabbing at my jaw line. We are in the middle of down town and surrounded by a number of tall buildings which could have launched the body down at us. They reach like mortar golems standing defiant against the red smeared sky. Black smoke billows weakly from a few windows. A tattered banner that reads 'HELP' flaps against the wall of the building next to us connected to only one of the two windows it was hung from. The window it is no longer attached to is shattered.

For some reason I think it might be where it fell from. I point dumbly up at the banner and Lila gives it an angry five second glare before turning her furious eyes back to me. She holds her hands at her sides curled into claws. Her long neglected finger nails are chipped and broken but form deadly talons I have no desire to tangle with. I just want a fucking Worm and now Lila wants to fight. Fights between Wormers are never casual affairs.

"If I said I was sorry would you calm down?" I ask in the most sympathetic voice my apathy allows.

"Are you?" She growls at me.

"I don't want to fight."

"Then say it?" She scolds.

"Say what?"

"Tell me you're fucking sorry."

"Okay, I'm sorry. Feel better?"

She turns back around in a huff but the murderous shine leaves her eyes. She wants to get high worse than she wants to fight and I don't blame her for it.

Plus, the exploding body may have something left close to its shredded form we can use in our journey to the local cemetery. We don't discuss this but we both think the same thought and lean closer to the gore pile. Life would be easy if you found things like you do in video games; piles of gold, ammo for whatever weapon you've secured from a lower level, handy heath packets that can keep you alive no matter what attacks you. Instead we kneel next to the mess and stick our hands into the pulped corpse searching for anything of use. Lila pulls a smashed cell phone from scraps of fabric that used to be a dirty pair of jeans. She regards the broken LCD screen and tosses it over her shoulder where it cracks in half on the concrete.

I find a Bic lighter in a similar scrap of jeans. I wipe it clean on my filthy shirt and take slight notice of the shape of a scowling face the stain leaves. I hold the lighter up in front of me and strike the wheel. Once, nothing. Twice, nothing. On the third strike a flame sparks to life at the tip. We both smile weakly at the flickering fire and I take my thumb away to save whatever fluid remains. A means of fire comes in handy in the new primitive world. I tuck it into my pocket, satisfied and ready to move along. Lila rolls a chunk of flattened meat to the side and digs in the back pockets while I lean closer to the dead man's face on the remarkably intact head.

I can tell it was a man because the chin is covered in whiskery shadow. Malformed by the force of the fall, the forehead bulges out at me obscenely. One eyeball hangs by strings of sinew and rests against the swollen cheek. The other is empty, likely somewhere behind me, expelled by the force of the landing. The mouth hangs open reveling long neglected teeth and bloody gums. Several teeth have streaks of glowing colors swirling with the decay. This bastard was eating the Worms.

"I found a kit," Lila says distracting me from the grotesque face.

Then, after ripping it open and examining the contents, "Damn it all, no Worms. Every rig is shattered."

I want to tell her of course that there are no fucking Worms; he was fucking eating them as well as shooting them. Of course every rig is broken. No shit, you dumb bitch, he fell from the sky and exploded on the sidewalk but instead I say, "Like so many dreams."

She smiles and tosses the useless kit over her shoulder to join the equally useless phone. Glass shards drop from the bag as it soars and the hollow sounds of them raining down echo off the buildings around us. We both take simultaneous deep breathes as if we realize what a tomb the city has become at exactly the same time. Next we hear intense thudding coming from one of the nearby buildings. It sounds like a building tearing itself apart from the inside but as the sounds get louder savage shouts join in the racket and we realize it is someone crashing down a stair well.

Lila dives back to the body to continue her morbid search while I scan the buildings trying in vain to narrow down where the thudding and screaming is originating.

"Holy shit!" Lila exclaims and sticks her hands into where I imagine the man's stomach used to be. She frantically wipes away chucks of gore to reveal what looks like a bent black bone next to his shattered spine. She wraps her fingers around it and tugs but in doesn't budge. Her hand slips off it and she grabs it with both hands. She looks like she is about to give the rudest-hand-job-ever to a chunk of decayed bone. Both hands slip away and she yells 'FUCK' in frustration.

"It must have been tucked into the back of his pants when he fell." She tells me while kung fu gripping it a second time.

I look at her, confused and distracted, as the clatter draws ever closer.

"What the hell are you doing?" I ask as the furious sounds crescendo with the shattering of a plate glass window to the building with the HELP banner. An almost forgotten emotion (pride, maybe) rises inside of me at my correct assumption as to where the body fell from. The emancipated form of a rail thin man in a paisley print muumuu leaps through the shattered window and lands in an awkward heap on the ground.

With a growling tug and the resounding crack of bone, Lila removes a gore slick hand gun from the body. The momentum from her tug sends her to her ass where she holds up the weapon. When I look at her the crimson covered pistol in front of her face is blurry as the glow in her eyes steals all my focus.

CHAPTER FOUR

OUR DAY IS GETTING INCREASINGLY CHAOTIC.

The crumpled pile of bright paisley print muumuu and shards of glass moans as the man struggles to his feet. The larger pieces of glass slide off him and shatter on the concrete, smaller pieces stick in the flesh of his taunt cheeks and forearms or leave bright red scratches that color coordinate well with his vibrant muumuu. He staggers in a small semi-circle gathering his bearings. He wears one tattered bunny slipper missing both eyes and one ear. On his other foot is an old high-top sneaker.

He slaps himself, hard, in his face. At his feet is what looks to be an old baseball bat with nine-inch-nails driven through the end to form a homemade Morning Star mace. He shouts, "The bastards are upon us! Leave the lamps but grab the regret!"

Then he notices us.

"Carl! There're right here! Carl!" He screams over his shoulder as if more people are behind him.

We see or hear no such people.

He kneels down and picks up his bat weapon. While he does, Lila tucks the gun under her legs to keep it a secret. He holds the bat in front of him like a sword and shouts over his shoulder again, "Goddamn it, Carl! Get your ass down here!"

I take a slow step towards Lila while keeping my eyes on him and his brutal looking toy. The man takes a slow step closer to me, the wind causing his brightly colored muumuu to wave like he wrapped himself in a neon flag. I inch towards Lila, he inches towards me. I take a step, he takes a step. The lone ear on his bunny slipper flops with each of his movements.

Once I'm close to Lila I reach a hand down to her and help her to her feet. I try to pull my hand back and she squeezes it with both of her hands. The man finally notices the pulped body between us. His eyes grow big at the morbid site.

"Carl!" He screams over his shoulder, "It's serious, they know about the plan!"

We stare at him nervous as to what to do. We are ready to leave but you never turn your back on a Wormer; especially a Wormer with a bat as mean looking as his. He takes another step, looking from us to the corpse puddle and back again.

He turns all the way around and yells with enough force blood mists in the air by his mouth, "Goddamn it, Carl!"

"C'mon." I whisper to Lila and tug her in the direction of the graveyard.

His head snaps back to us eyes watering with panic and confusion but not glowing yet. His adrenaline is mixing with whatever chemicals the Worms leave inside of us as they dissolve into murderous bliss. His bloodshot eyes return to the splattered corpse. Recognition fogs his eyes but it has to fight the glowing sheen already forming in the corner of his eyes. He shakes his head violently, slapping himself hard across his face with one hand. I keep my eyes on his other hand still clutching tight his club.

I think for a second he is going to break into a sobbing fit. He proves my thought wrong and snarls while raising the weapon above his head. I play the part of concerned lover and shove Lila further behind me. I reach my arm behind me in the wild hope that she hands me the hand gun. She doesn't even notice. She is staring at the man standing knock kneed with the wind blowing his neon muumuu and his club held shakily aloft.

"That's Carl." He says his eyes fixed on the gore.

I don't know if he is asking a question or if he is introducing us to the exploded donor of our new pistol. I say nothing but take a slow step back that gets me close enough to nudge Lila again. Her body feels anchored to the ground by her feet and curiosity. She bounces the gun back and forth of the back of her leg like a twitch more than a conscious thought.

The man's face contorts into a murderous scowl and I see the same glowing stains on his half rotted teeth. His knees snap back into posture and squat. He howls and runs towards Carl, muumuu flapping, with his club held samurai like above him like Ito Ogami's worse nightmare. Instinct and self-preservation moves me backwards with enough force Lila has no choice but to move as well.

The man swings the club down with remarkable force for such a malnourished example of Wormer. Carl's lumpy head bursts on impact. Rather than exploding, the thick gout of blood shoots from his ear and his head quickly unfurls like a self-peeling orange. He gives it a second whack as forceful as the first and the skull chips away revealing chunky gray matter swimming with neon Worms.

My mouth goes dry and my dick gets hard at the sight of the Worms. Lila groans with longing and she tries to push me aside. The feeling that something is dreadfully wrong rages strong against my craving trying to choke the sexual thrill out of it. I elbow her in the chest to back her away from the body while taking another step back myself.

The man in the muumuu drops his club next to the corpse and howls in triumph. He fist pumps once and begins digging through the brain gore for the Worms. At first I don't see what makes these Worms different than the ones I want dissolving inside me. They glow and squirm the same, yet something about them raise the hair on the back of my neck. Lila grunts and shoves me again-harder this time- so I back her up with a harder elbow to keep us even.

Then as the man snags a Worm between his finger and thumb I see the difference. The Worms, normally featureless and smooth, have tiny pained faces and rows of small spines running the length of their squirming forms. The man holds the worm tight between his grubby fingers and it opens a tiny mouth filled with needle sharp teeth and squeals. The grin that parts the man's mouth makes my empty stomach roll.

The squeal gives Lila pause long enough she sees the mutated worm. She gasps and stops shoving me forward. Her gasp catches the man's attention. His eyes shine when he looks at us, drool dripping from his chapped lips.

Still holding the squealing squirming worm he nods at the corpse, "This is Carl. Carl is dead now."

"We didn't do it," I tell him dumbly, "he fell from up there."

"I know. I pushed him." His scowl fades and he wheezes a laugh. Strangely enough the neon sheen over his wise eyes remains. "He made a big fucking mess, eh?"

The man smiles past us, as the worm twitches and rolls against his pinching fingers, his eyes reflecting neon sheen. His smile cracks with a sob, he struggles to rebuild it, but a river of tears destroys the feeble grin.

"He was my best friend." The man in the muumuu wipes bloody snot on the stretched sleeve of his vibrant house dress. "A right proper buddy. He was best at billiards and I was better at bowling. We were about the same at burning down trailers. Yup, tell yer friends Carl and Tuck was as thick as thieves in quicksand. But, I didn't have no choice 'bout it though. I was sure the Worms got into his skull," he holds up the mutated worm, "and I was fuckin' right."

Lila's finger nails are digging into the soft flesh of my arm. Small streams of blood trickle off my elbow. Her eyes are fixed on the dangerously looking worm-so much sharper than their slick backed brethren. The steady sting of her nails piercing my flesh in jagged crescents keeps my head clearer than normal. The Worm holds little sway over me. However Carl's murderous friend finishes his hiccup eulogy and his glowing eyes dart back to the tiny neon pink monster worm.

Silence crowds close around us; a buzzing silence amplified by the tall buildings and empty streets. It hums and builds like a hive chattering towards Armageddon. Other Worms burrowing through Carl's pulpy gray matter squeal as they are exposed to the poisoned air and the black sunshine. Tuck slaps at his ear. Once, twice, and then he opens his mouth and dangles the Worm above his open jaw. My eyes blur from his noxious corpse pit breath. Lila squeezes my arm again, digging her talons into tender flesh and muscle.

Pain, paranoia, disgust, and withdraw wrap me tight and squeeze a cry from me.

"FUCK!"

I yell it at Lila and her dagger finger nails.

I yell it at the Carl stain delaying our cemetery visit.

I yell it at the fact the cemetery is the only place I want to go, for many reasons.

I yell it at the empty streets.

I yell it at the Worm addicted citizens lurking in the shadows.

I yell it at satellite-video cameras left master-less to document Armageddon.

I yell it at humankind; so flawed and inventive, so violent and self-important.

I yell it at the Worms; so honest, so treacherous, so malevolent.

I yell it at broken glass and fractured dreams.

I yell it at the rubble.

I yell it at burnt out bulbs and hospitals.

I yell it at the rot.

I yell it at the neon death choking the world.

I yell it at Tuck; the Worm mere inches from his sarlacc-pitted mouth.

Only Tuck responds in the least. He closes his mouth and tilts his head at me like a confused dog. His tooth-remiss-grin cracks his weathered face. He opens his mouth to talk. His mouth a cave, opened like a bullhorn, but before sound can leave his throat the worm raises the tiny razor spikes on its hide. They slice through Tuck's thumb flesh with predatory quickness. Droplets of tainted blood hang in the air while the mutant Worm wiggles free and snaps its rows of tiny teeth at the corner of Tuck's left eye. Gnashing needle fangs shred soft jaundiced eye flesh. The Worm wiggles its swollen body into the wound and it uses the spikes on its hide to slither lightning fast to Tuck's Worm warped brain. The remains of Tuck's eyeball split jaggedly in half as the Worm's ass-end waves once and disappears in gore. The drops of blood from Tuck's initial thumb wound splatter the concrete.

Tuck slaps at his destroyed eye. With his equilibrium equally as destroyed, he falls backwards screaming nonsensical curse words.

I take the attack as a chance to escape the situation. The mutant Worms don't appeal to me (yet) so better not to push (hope). I will seek my normal glowing Worms sleek and lustrous, merciful in their destruction.

Lila stands in place when I walk past. She turns to face me, slivers of a rainbow sheen dancing across her pale vacant eyes. She says nothing but jerks her thumb silently in the direction of Carl's Worm-farm pulp. Tuck, who has been rolling back and forth frothing choked words into his frail wrists, suddenly leaps to his feet at her gesture. He turns to face us. Glowing pink pus leaks down his face onto his muumuu from his seeping eye crater. He has his club in one twitchy hand, the other held up covering the wounded left side of his face and mouth.

The right side of his grin turns up and spreads wide. The top half of the grin fractures with a wet crack and adjusts to something separating the bones and then filling them solid with something else. Glowing shards of bone slice down through his blackened gums, pulverizing Tuck's two remaining teeth. He catches the shards of rotted teeth on his tongue and he swallows them.

Tangles of chemical reeking blood dangle off his chin as he takes a wobbly step towards us. He pulls his hand away from his wound, revealing a black crusted scab dripping glowing ichors down his cheek. His mouth has taken on a snout-ish appearance due to the extra bone growth above his mouth. More blood drips from the glowing bone shard teeth lining Tuck's upper gums.

"I knew you'd make a play for my Worms, you have the junkie eyes." His remaining eye, a glowing ball of rainbow fury, claws at Lila. Finally she becomes unsettled enough to move her ass. She backs away from him but refuses to turn her back on him so the escape is slow.

He dashes forward, raising the bludgeon as he approaches. Lila falls to her ass. As she rocks back, she raises Carl's handgun. The blast is deafening, amplified and echoed by the vacant buildings. More so for Tuck as the bullet hits him in his cheek, shatters his cheek bone, and careens through skull meat to explode out the back of his head. The skinny man staggers sideways. His club falls to the ground followed immediately by his muumuu covered knees. His head tips forward on his thin chest, so his corpse mourns the Carl stain in front of it.

Howls and moans rise on the foul wind, Wormers shaken from their highs by the reverberating sound of gunfire. Without speaking a word, we grab each other's hands and walk around Tuck and Carl giving the diseased corpses a wide berth. As we pass curiosity dictates I glance at the crater in the back of Tuck's skull. As I suspected thick, spiny luminescent Worms burrow through the splattered gray matter.

CHAPTER FIVE

THERE ARE ONLY SIMPLE CHOICES IN A DEAD WORLD.

There are two graveyards in town. One has been walled in by The Church of the Dying Star, proclaimed the Temple, and is heavily guarded by the fanatics. The cult is still comprised of many men of science and the few humans resistant to the worm's neon call still, perhaps rightfully, blame these men. The Church is as easily as heavily armed as their detractors, not to mention the insanity the long time Wormers surely share. Every temple they've built (or stolen) has eventually become a war zone; save for the one downtown.

The other graveyard has been cordoned off by different Diggers, each with his own army of Grave-savers or armed thugs, and each supplies the dwindling populace's addiction. It is rare to ever find the same Digger more than once or twice. The control of the grave dirt is a never ending struggle for the damned. The fertile mud is thick with junkie blood. The Church's Temple graveyard is much closer by at least twelve city blocks, but all we got left is our poisoned time. The community graveyard is on the other side of town, the old side that fell first, and it lies beyond a deadly maze of deserted city streets and shadowed parks. That's the one that has our number.

We will keep the gun. Five bullets left and each is a solution of to a problem. The first solved the problem of what to do with a crazed and murderous Tuck. I have the snarling gut feeling we'll use them all before our craving is sated.

CHAPTER SIX

WE DON'T TRUST THE NOISE AND WE DON'T TRUST THE SILENCE.

I hear them. I hear them scampering down barren flights of stairs, groaning from pitch black alley way homes, and whooping rape cries as they chase the echoing gun report like hobo knights hunting a smoke dragon. We don't have time for any more distractions. As my adrenaline fades my crash makes a thunderous return darker and more painful than ever.

My stomach clenches. A sharp thudding pain on the left side of my chest slows my quick resolute steps to dragging stumbles. My soul is burning, perspiring the former me out in sulfuric iodine-colored sweat that stings my eyes as it runs down my face. My limbs go cold. I feel the hollowness. I feel eaten by Worms.

My vision blurs and illuminates in warping intervals rendering walking impossible. I slip to my knees. I feel fire in my lungs; it tickles with napalm fingers up my throat with every quivering breath. I know the only thing that can stop the horrendous withdraw. I focus all my mental energy in the squirming leech shape of a worm; slimy and luminescent and blessedly terminal. My eyes roll back in their sockets then fall forward landing on the hand gun tight in my white knuckled grip.

When did I get the gun?

I see Lila staggering away from me. Her arms are wrapped tight around herself in comfort. She gives herself the caring hug I am incapable of as she slowly, unknowingly, leaves me behind.

My eyes drift from her swaying ass to the handgun. My eyes refuse to focus enough to read the brand name etched on the weapon's smooth barrel. Too blurry. Too fuzzy. The tip of the gun suddenly glows a spectacular violet.

I am surrounded by the slow angry hiss and clunk of hydraulics.

The glowing purple tip squirms as if it conspires to wriggle away from the cold steel.

Out of the corner of my eye I see Lila freeze in place then cast a panicked glare my way.

The tip melts into the shape of a worm. My craving burns and sweats my memories away.

I can't take my eyes off the worm wiggling on the end of the gun but I hear Lila scream over the encroaching sound of creaking hydraulics as if my head is submerged in water.

My hand floats the worm barrel to my lips. I open my mouth and taste the chlorine and sugar syrup tang I'd always imagined the Worms would possess. I close my eyes as the smooth slimy worm slithers on my sandpaper dry tongue. I hear Lila screaming. I can't make out her words but I can imagine the jealous rage she is feeling over me getting the only worm. The hydraulic thunder is close and it is deafening. I hear more than one machine. The rapid crackle of machine gun fire shatters the illusion I'm holding. I'm kneeling in an alleyway with a gun barrel in my mouth. My eyes finally begin to focus. I stand back up just in time for Lila to tackle me back down with a shoulder to my ribs.

My head bounces off the filthy concrete with enough force that my vision goes incredibly bright.

It crinkles away like burning paper, revealing the hellish reality of my surroundings when the pain from the gun barrel shattering half the remaining teeth I have cuts through everything with resounding clarity. I try to scream but I gag on gun barrel, blood, and shards of broken teeth.

Lila jerks the gun from my mouth, spattering her chest with tooth-speckled blood. I imagine jerking the gun back away and putting one in her forehead, spattering my chest with skull speckled blood.

She holds a quivering finger to her lips while her eyes plead my understanding and silence.

Then I see the man-machines behind the racket. Two cyborg survivors thunder through the street at the end of the alley way followed by a few others slinking after on foot.

We've seen the cyborgs before in our lackadaisically lethal travels. The cyborgs are huge ghastly golems of metal and flesh bearing a closer resemblance to a medieval torture device than a Star Trek villain. Strands of barbed wire zigzag the exposed flesh of the host human forever tearing new gushing wounds through thick layers of scar tissue while holding them in place atop their robot battle suits. Wires and rods disappear under blackened necrotic tissue. A mass of multi-colored wires run from the metal shells to gaping holes in the back of the human heads. They've sacrificed their hands and feet, scorched black bone melds with robotic extensions of their former limbs. They stop at the mouth of the alley way, standing on either side of Carl and Tuck, and the Immunie soldiers surrounding them are awaiting orders. Fresh craters speckle Tuck, each smoking from the hot chunk of lead sizzling in his dead flesh.

"Aside from the shots fired by Rodoon, One shot, one wound." A foot solider with a graying flat-top hair cut says to the cyborgs. He gives Tuck's muumuu clad corpse a quick careful pat down before kicking it over into the Carl-puddle.

"Whoever fired the shot is still close." The cyborg known as Rodoon announces in a voice like screaming glass.

"Search the vicinity," The second, Mafint, orders in a more mechanized voice, "You two down the store fronts, you two down the alley across the street, and you two down this alley here."

We shrink closer together behind the burned out remains of a dumpster as two of the troopers begin walking towards us guns held high. The cyborgs crowd around the gray haired soldier, who rests on his feet as he jabs a survival knife into Tuck's splattered gray matter. He jumps in surprise, pin-wheeling his arms (and the long jagged blade) as he steps up and away from

Tuck's blasted cranium. The cyborgs laugh, a hideous soulless robotronic pulse. The two Immunies walking in our direction turn away from our hiding place as they look to the laughing cyborgs.

"It's not funny." The officer scolds the machine-men. "Both these Wormers have the W-Gen 3 digging through their brain meat."

The cyborg laughter winds down like a siren sinking in sludge.

"Sorry, Sergeant Stan," Mafint says, his voice a whirling whine.

Sgt. Stan's square jaw grinds and pops as he storms over to Rodoon's side. The cyborg's human face looks tiny with the massive machine gun torrents welded to his robotic back and shoulders. I can't get a great view of his facial expression; I believe it is something between a bitter pout and a murderous scowl. Sgt. Stan types in a code on a key pad on Rodoon's giant metal leg. With a hiss and creak a small metal panel slides down opening a hidden compartment. He reaches in and retrieves a small rack of glass vials. He examines the tubes quickly then reaches back into the compartment for a pair of stainless steel tongs. Satisfied, he re-storms to Tuck's side. He kneels and jabs the tongs into reeking meat. He digs a bright glowing blue worm, identical to the one that burrowed into Tuck's eye, from the pulp. His square jaws pops as he deposits the hideous spiked beast into one of the glass tubes.

The soldiers in our alley stand transfixed on their superiors. I realize our chance to flee is upon us. Lila looks at me, her frozen eyes agreeing with my silent thoughts. We hold hands. Our sensation of touch is ravaged, pleasurable only when Worm-high and the sensation of flesh on flesh itches like wet sandpaper. We crouch-waddle along the moss covered wall behind the soldiers towards the back door to the building.

Sgt. Stan continues his morbid task until each vial carries a squirming squealing Worm. His men stare unmoving, we move an inch at a time in the shadow of their ignorance. Sgt. Stan holds the rack of vials up so the poisoned sunlight shines through the Worms' prickly bodies.

"Decontaminate them, Mafint. Then we'll find the one that did this. They might be infected as well." The Sarge's square jaw clicks and pops as he talks. His wide eyes never leave the illuminated Worm-flesh trapped in his tubes.

Mafint nods his tiny human head and his machine legs creak, hiss, and clack to life. His sturdy metal legs cover distance with robotic ease and in a single step he towers above the worm-ridden corpses. He points his left arm. I can see where the fractured and decayed bones of his forearm meld into the smooth metal of the flamethrower cylinder attachment. Thick black hoses connect to fittings planted in the flesh of his bicep and wrap around to two large tanks on his wide metal back. The hoses swing and sway as if they are suddenly filled with something. Then a ball of fire erupts from the end of the torch-arm engulfing the two corpses in white hot flames. The thin fabric of Tuck's muumuu turns to brittle ash. Immediately following his wardrobe, his pale skin blisters and peels away from muscles that turn pitch black as the flame licks Tuck's body with its thousands of fiery tongues. The muscles melt away in an instant and his skeleton suffers the same fate. The Carl puddle boils thick spurting bubbles that crust to the pavement before glazing shimmering colors in the incinerated pulped innards.

The intense temperature from the flamethrower heats the air until it is wavy, prismatic, and blurry. Just a few scant feet from the doorway Sgt. Stan spots us through the heat haze sneaking away from his men. The force of his command sends shivers through the blurs.

"GET THEM!"

His men spin on their heels and start firing before they even see us. Bullets shred the dumpster we were just hiding behind. The aroma of gun powder and scorched metal pursues us through the door. We scamper inside the darkened building, panicked and blind, as bullets pelt the swinging metal door behind us.

We crawl-dash over destroyed wooden furniture through the first room and are standing by the time we reach the next door. We swing it wide open and we are in a hallway lit with the strange sunlight that stabs through the boards covering the windows. Opposite the boarded up windows the wall is lined with doors; some open, some closed, and some just plain fucking gone. We hear the two soldiers a they crash through the first door as we are halfway down the hallway. The hissing and clanking of the cyborg's hydraulics clatters so loud we hear it as we reach the end of the hallway. Bullets follow us through the next door as well.

We end up in a stairwell instead of a room and our momentum nearly sends Lila over the handrail. I grab her by the back of her shirt and her hair and tug her back into my arms. I shove her up the stairs and follow inches from her ass, scampering up them on all fours like a beast.

Our pursuers repeat our mistake and crash into the hand rail. Except I'm guessing their gas masks obstruct the already dismally lit stairwell, because the one that hit second crashes into his partner so hard and fast he couldn't have grabbed him if he had wanted to. Gas mask muffled screams cut short with a crack and a thud.

Lila slips and I crawl right over her to the landing at the second floor. The hallway is well enough lit through a big metal door, a large glass square, obviously used to take up most of the upper half of the door. I imagine it had chicken wire and put up a hell of a fight. Beyond the gapping door hole unnatural sun light shines through unblocked windows on a room littered with a dozen or so Wormers lost in the throng of Worm-high. A man sits on a chair in the entrance way. Two girls kneel before him each stroking his cock into the others mouths while he rolls his eyes and thrusts his hips at their gags. My stomach clenches and my dick throbs with jealousy, not for the two headed blow job but for the Worm coursing through their systems. We may have been here before. I almost shout it to Lila before remembering I had just trampled her and left her on the stairs only twenty steps from a Worm immune soldier.

CHAPTER SEVEN

THE WORM IMMUNE (IMMUNIES) HAD TO WATCH ALL THEIR FRIENDS AND FAMILIES SUCCUMB TO THE CALL OF THE WORMS.

They were the ones that tried in vain to warn the leaders we were falling to the strange iridescent Worms. They were the ones that pulled the big ass #8 sized needles required to shoot the Worms from the cold stiff fingered grasps of six-year-olds. They were the ones that begged and pleaded with Worm crazed lovers until the Wormer would cram a screwdriver into their own ears. They were the ones searching for abandoned relatives in abandoned hospitals housing murderous junkies instead of doctors and nurses. They were the ones that sought shelter in the imagined safety of churches only to be gang-raped by a congregation of Wormers. They bore witness to the gore orgies of fallen cities lost in glowing sin and decay. They watched us slit our wrists and let the blood flow through our filthy fingers. They were the ones that watched everyone die.

Their angst and fury is universal. They suffer no further survival of the Worms or Wormers.

CHAPTER EIGHT

LILA IS RATHER QUICK THINKING FOR SUCH A DEVILISH BITCH.

The Immunie soldier leans over the railing, staring into the murky basement darkness that claimed his friend. His head snaps up towards us catching us in his baleful glare. His eyes twitch behind the lens of his gas mask as he raises his weapon.

"You two! Don't fucking move!" The gas mask muffles his voice but I can still hear his anger.

Lila raises our gun and squeezes the trigger twice.

Fire and metal explode from the barrel and in the flash light of destruction we see the bullets tear into the soldier. One hits his hip and cleaves away muscle, flesh and pocket as it careens into the wall behind him. The other bullet lodges firmly a half inch under his belt buckle. The lighting strikes of gunfire leave our tired eyes seeing explosions of Technicolor in the dim of the hallway. We don't see him fall but we hear his muffled screams.

I reach down and grab my blood-crazed girlfriend by her shoulders to tug her up the stairs. Instead I find her rooted to the spot. At first, I think her mind has finally slipped. Her brain likes hearing the gunshot. It could be her new addiction. Then she grabs my hand on her shoulder with a cold clammy hand of her own. She gives me a gentle but forceful tug and I react by trying to jerk my arm away from her crazy ass as hard as possible. She holds the pistol to her lips and silences my fight. She leans in and whispers in my ear.

"He thinks we'll hide upstairs. We can sneak past him and escape through the basement level."

I wager one last desirous glare towards the blissfully unaware Wormers on the second floor. One of the women has perched her emancipated frame on the girth of the man's prick and the two buck and thrust in very different grooves. The second woman kneels between both with a finger third knuckle deep in each of their asses. In the reverberating echo of the gun I hear the tortured screams of the crash from the large room behind the threesome. If there was more Worms to be had we wouldn't hear the scream. No one can handle the first peeling edges of the high fleeing. The synthetic bliss of the building is about to be shattered whether we lead a troop of armed Immunies through it or not. Lila is right, of course, there is no escape once we climb the stairs.

So we slither-slink back down them. We reach the landing, and are very careful to step in between the wounded man's prone legs. He groans and whimpers tears and sweat mixing under the dense rubber of his gas mask, every breath birthing a fresh spurt of blood from his abdomen. I marvel at the steady drip of his blood down the stairs as his destroyed bowels lose control for the last time.

We reach the first stair in our descent and we hear the cyborgs smashing their way into the building. The ear-splitting hiss and creak of their movement is nothing compared to the roar of the walls being smashed as they clatter towards us. Lila crawls over the Immunie broken on the stairs kneeing him in his dead balls and chin as she passes. I attempt a sliding escape with the hopes of using the corpse as a speed ramp of sorts. Instead my flip flop slips in the growing river of blood, piss and shit and I land directly on top of it.

The door to the stairwell is blown off its hinges. A cloud of dust envelops the corpse and I. The wounded Immunie above screams obscenities behind his death tasting mask. The dust, flakes of splintered metal, is drawn to the damp of his gushing wound where it will cake and itch.

I hear them above me and know Lila is lost in the shadows below. No time to hide, I roll the dead man on top of me. The wounded soldier's gas mask hits the wall and tumbles down the stairs past me and my corpse shield.

"Where is Tadarou?" Sgt. Stan's voice is stoic and steady.

The soldier screams his answer through clenched teeth, "Down…stairs."

"Where are the Wormers?"

The soldier's voice creaks as impending death impedes his words, "Up…stairs."

"All right." Sgt. Stan grunts his satisfaction. "Rodoon, thank him for his service."

I hear the ominous creak and hiss of the massive cyborg drawing close. Then, in his high pitched whine, "The Cause recognizes you as a soldier and therefore regrets your demise. Your service has been appreciated."

The burst of bullets Rodoon unleashes from his arm cannon reduces the soldier to shreds and small pulpy mounds in a matter of seconds. I use the thunderous chatter as cover and slide down the stairs covered in the dead man's gore. I manage to grab the machine gun from the soldier on top of me as I glide past him into the shadows of the basement.

CHAPTER NINE

WE HAVE LEVELED UP.

We scamper away from the stairs with our hands on the wall. The darkness is absolute and the solid of the concrete wall gives us the necessary anchor to reality we need to judge movement and direction and space. We hear the echoes of the soldier's foot falls as they ascend to the second floor and the unfortunate Wormers tripping there. The robotic clatter of Rodoon and Mafint following is over-powered by the sounds of the sudden massacre. Even with the vacant floor between us the reverberation of shrieks and automatic weapon fire dances around us from every direction as if gun casings should be raining down upon us and the walls are howling their death throes into our scraped palms.

We inch through the darkness, communication rendered null due to the sounds of slaughter above, and our minds are wracked with adrenaline and worm craving. The blackness of the dark is so dense and physical my mind starts seeing horrible colors swirling all around. I see amorphous monsters and American Dream regret churning in the sinister gloom; snapping, fucking, killing and dying. I count the number of bullets in Lila's handgun in my head to keep my mind busy.

One for Tuck. *(Focus, mother fucker)*

Two for the Immunie above us. *(Poor bastard never felt the needle-sharp pang of the need or the razor blade ecstasy of the high.)*

Three left. *(That's at least one for me and a matching one for her.)*

Romance at the end of the world is simply not dying alone.

I slowly realize the strange smooth weight in my right hand. My memories struggle past the thunder of gun fire and the thick mental haze of worm craving. I stole the Immunie's machine gun. I have enough bullets to solve any problem in our way. We reach a corner in the pitch black room and Lila leans her head on my chest. She turns her face to me in the darkness and I smell her breath, like candy and rot, thick in my nostrils. I can't wrap my arm around her because of my new weapon so I lean down and kiss my chapped lips to her cold-sweaty forehead. She shivers against me, the vibrations of her body jumping to me like electric currents and making me shiver in response.

The chatter of gunfire dies slowly but the echo of the massacre radiates through the entire building giving us another shared shiver. We hear the floor creak as the men and cyborgs search through the carnage for us. I know Sgt. Stan got a good look at us. He'll realize we aren't among the bullet ridden corpses and he'll keep looking for us. His sense of justice is as demented as a Wormer's sense of contentment.

"We can't stay here," I whisper to Lila. My dry throat drinks the words the first time I try to speak them like shards of glass through quick-sand. I swallow the lump of trepidation and say it again louder.

She doesn't say anything. Her shiver mutates into a steady tremble.

"Lila, we can't stay here!" I say it louder than I mean to and she pushes away from me with the hand holding her pistol. The butt of it digs into my chest and I wince with pain and instant regret for the volume of my voice. It could be the panic and the guns, it could be the darkness and the bright swirling monsters there, or maybe it's yet another side-effect of main-lining the glowing creatures.

"There!" Someone shouts in the dense gloom behind us.

A beam of light clicks on. It blinds us with its all-illuminating glare. Immediately following its birth is a hail of gunfire in our direction. We duck under the beam and waddle-run away from the bullet ridden corner. Through the high ringing in my ears I hear the cyborgs above racing towards the stairs.

That Sgt. Stan is one smart twisted fuck. He sent a few of his men down the stairs anyways. They stalked behind us, their flashlight and gun held at the ready. They heard the same sounds of their team slaughtering the room full of Wormer's and now they were feeling the craving for a kill. As my own craving jolts me forward I realize it is my sense of self-preservation; the only reason I flee from their weapons instead of opening my arms wide and welcoming the hot spurts of metallic death they offer. They exist only to kill Wormers, so it must be what they crave. As the beam of light searches for our hunched moving shapes the gun chatters random shots in different directions. I suddenly feel like we could almost understand each other. We won't. That's not how humans work anymore.

With each burst of gunfire the bright flashes from the barrel illuminate the soldier and reflect in the lens of his gas mask. Lila must notice as well because the next time the soldier fires she gambles another bullet while running like a crazy hunchbacked bitch through a dark dungeon of a basement. The shot is frighteningly accurate smashing through the mask's filtering system before the soldier's mouth. He falls backwards, firing bullets into the ceiling and gurgling his death rattle.

We hear the other soldier speak into a walkie-talkie as he searches for us even more franticly with his shaking beam.

"Man down! Targets are in the basement! Man down!"

We follow the next wall until it turns to the left finally granting us some cover. We hear a crackling mechanical answer to the soldier's message but I don't understand the words. We hear the cyborgs storm into the dark of the basement. The next instant Mafint blows a stream of blue-hot flame into the ceiling. The quaky light from the flames reaches for us and illuminates the shapes of Mafint, Rodoon, and Sgt. Stan. From where we hide in the shadows, the soldier stands between us and them. He waves in our direction and Sgt. Stan nods back. Rodoon raises both his gun torrent arms and fires. Fat shadowy chunks of silhouetted soldier explode away from him as the large caliber bullets shred him in their hot blind pursuit of us. We duck and run until we finally reach a set of heavy double doors. We shove the release bars but they have sat unused for so long rust has taken over the internal mechanism and they don't budge.

Rodoon holds his fire and we hear them walking towards the turn in the wall. The fire Mafint lit is spreading across the mold caked ceiling at an incredible speed, and it is illuminating everything in its hungry glare. Once they round the corner we are dead. And then I remember the smooth deadly weight of the machine gun. I lie on my stomach on the floor and wait while Lila throws her lithe frame repeatedly against the rusted stubborn doors.

Rodoon is the first one that walks into my sights. I pull the trigger, with a finger stiff with craving, and light him up from his crotch to his ugly scarred face. He screams in a voice crackling with humanity as fist-sized holes punch their way up his torso. Blood and oil explode from the points of impact in greasy pulpy wads. His human form convulses as his organs are ripped apart by hot lead and his mechanical limbs fire sporadic bursts of gun fire while the legs lean back impossibly far and kick franticly. A burst of random death-twitch fire explodes above me and Lila drops to the filthy ground beside me. The high caliber bullets do the job and peel the doors from their rusted hinges.

Lila jumps up and dives through the blasted open doors as Sgt. Stan, Mafint, and the last two soldiers wearing gas masks approach a dying Rodoon. Their eyes are drawn to the chaos that is Rodoon's demise. Before following Lila through the door to the freedom beyond, I point at the group and pull the trigger.

CHAPTER TEN

THICK BLACK SMOKE OOZES FROM BETWEEN THE BOARDED-UP WINDOWS OF THE FIRST FLOOR.

We dash through it, breathe it in, and spit up ash once we reach a shell of a burnt out mini-van crashed just up the alleyway. Lila tries to run past it but I grab her frail wrist and jerk her back. The adrenaline and Worm craving have pushed her too far. Her eyes have a faint glow and I don't have time for it so I give her a quick hard gut shot with the butt of my new gun. She hunches over and crumbles next to the van where she quivers and foams slightly at her mouth. I lean next to her withdraw and get a good look back through the door we just exited.

The flaming ceiling is falling down in great blackened sections all around the Immunie patrol. When a thick glowing support beam swings down and crushes one of the two remaining soldiers with its fiery weight Mafint uses his flame thrower hands to shove sternly at Sgt. Stan who is try to open the compartment on Rodoon's leg. The cyborg manages to scoot the stubborn son of a bitch almost out the door before he pulls some kind of crazy football move and spins around the lumbering machine-man back to Rodoon's side.

Mafint squeals something in a harsh grind as he backs out the door. As his giant metal foot steps down, a gust of flames spits out the door propelled by the force of the first floor collapsing. The last remaining soldier sets his weapon against the wall and runs back into the inferno. He emerges seconds later dragging the charred, smoking, and leg-less form of Sgt. Stan. Clutched tight in the terribly disfigured but still living man's hands is the rack of glass vials; each containing a mutated glowing worm. The last soldier rips off his gas mask and lets it slip through his fingers while he stares speechless at his commanding officer. Crispy skin slides off of scorched muscles, and droops to the filthy floor, leaving Sgt. Stan a hideous gray-black-red blob twitching between life and death.

"Well done, soldier," Mafint whirs and clicks his emotionless compliment, "Consider yourself promoted. The Cause will now recognize you as an officer, Sgt. Sluka. You will owe the Cause as many kills as your noble blood will grant you. You owe the Cause your life because the Cause is the only way to achieve a future in the new dead world. Mother Lair has been notified of your promotion and your new responsibilities commence immediately. A new platoon has been dispatched and will meet us at Remote Lair 7.3. The Cause is proud to be owed your life, Sgt. Sluka. May your kills be many and your death worthy."

The cyborg finishes his droning speech and Sgt. Sluka picks up Sgt. Stan in his arms like a grief-stricken parent with a smoldering child. The building is spitting flames halfway to the penthouse. The decimated squad walks away from the blaze they started and head in the exact same direction we need to go to reach our graveyard goal and grab our prize.

I curse under my breath. My joints ache and the ache is spreading like liquid pain into my muscles. My vision blurs. I regain focus and then immediately lose it again. Black fuzzes the edge of my vision and it cracks and reaches like electricity. I curse more. I watch the slow exit of the three surviving Immunies in a blurry black and white. My stomach twists and knots threatening to drop me to my knees. My new gun will be worth fuck-all if I am curled up, covered in drool and shit, next to Lila. It would be game over.

The world is swirling, the end looming when someone speaks next to me.

"If yeh pass out, Billyshanks, I'm stealin' yer goon."

My head turns slowly, every inch an enormous chore, towards the familiar voice. My brain takes as long to process the words. The odd rhythm means someone I know is talking to me but my memory is a hazy ruin anymore.

When I see him I don't recognize him at first. He wears night vision goggles with everything except the lenses spray painted neon colors. Poker-chip-blue hair stretches off his head as if static powered and sentient. Thin matching rapist mustache sleazes under his crooked nose. Two pale blue Worm tattoos slither up his narrow cheeks, in the right dark light the Worms glow fierce neon blue. He wears turquoise necklaces like Mr. T wore gold chains and they obscure most of his thin chest. On his left hand is a filthy sock with three or four dozen googly eyes glued to it. Most are clustered at the tip and they all spin to stare at me.

My brain scrambles to piece together the puzzle as my eyes take all of him in. As familiar as this man is I can't summon any memory or detail. My body is ready to sway, my worthless mind will follow. My eyes roll back as gravity wraps around me. I feel the burn of vomit in my chest and throat. I give myself to the sway. I hear his voice as I rapidly fade.

"Well, 'tanks fer da goon, Billyshanks! Also, I could be takin' a stab at yer lady as yeh both be twitching it off…"

CHAPTER ELEVEN

WITHDRAWAL GAGS YOU, AND SOMETIMES YOUR INSIDES EAT THEMSELVES.

That was the fate I expected while the darkness was swallowing me. Once my bloodshot eyes opened, I almost squealed at my luck. We had run into Billy Shanks, the man we were gambling our lives to meet at the graveyard. He had moved us to some sort of wooded area that further confused me during my waking moments. He waited a few minutes for us to drool and convulse and sit up before we attempt conversation.

"Billy," I smile the most joyous grin I can muster and it feels like a snarl. "Got any Worms?"

"Ah, Billyshanks," he laughs with confidence, "I knew dat'd be yer firs' query. Not, 'Oi, Billy, where is mah goon?' or 'Say, Billy, yeh didn' get third knuckle deep on mah lady, did ja'?"

Lila rolls her blood-shot eyes back into her skull. She crosses her arms over her chest to cover her pert nipples pushing against the thin fabric. Whether he is joking (which is giving the word 'joke' a very wide berth) or not, he has always made her nervous. She tells me I make her feel safe.

I killed her ex-boyfriend Samson because I didn't like the way he shook her.

Maybe, Billy knows I'd kill him too if he shook her.

"Nah, I didn' finger her butt 'ole or plop mah dink in yer mouth 'ole," he affirms with a wave of his sock-puppet clad hand despite the chuckle he can't suppress. "And yer goon is right 'ere, Billyshanks. I recall da two of yeh. Yeh bring me soul stones," He jabs one long thumb at the layers of turquoise necklaces and then points the same thumb at me, "And yeh kilt Charlie Wizard. I owe yeh fer 'at, always will, Billyshanks."

The name punches me in the gut. My stomach cramps fingers of agony throughout my body. Memories flood my head. Regret blisters pop and drain over mental scar tissue. The depths I have sunk, how long I have wallowed in the murky foul deep as if I was born a creature of the abyss. I don't deny my guilt, but I do suppress it with tender glowing Worm flesh. With no Worms in the needle I have to gaze clearly upon the horrible head-fuck of reality. I can't fucking take it. No one can. No one can remain sane in the dead world. I choke every sour emotion down my dry throat and speak weakly through my chapped lips.

"Thanks for not raping us, Billy. And thanks for not stealing my new gun. But…"

"I ain't stole yer goon yet." He interrupts. I nod impatiently my guts threatening to revolt and steal my consciousness again.

"You got any Worms, Billy?"

"Well, kinda." He nods with both his head and sock-puppet clad hand.

"Billy, how the fuck do you 'kinda' have some Worms?" Lila's voice is strained, her teeth clenched back in her throat.

"Well, Billyshanks, I do 'ave some." He answers her while nodding his sock-puppet. Then he waves it in a big circle around him drawing our attention to the tall trees that have replaced the colossal eerie buildings that formally surrounded us. "Jus' not' 'ere."

"Well, where the fuck are your Worms then, Billy?" Lila's frustration is raising the pitch of her whining voice like a kettle left to boil out.

I'm distracted by the thick coverage of the leafless branches of the towering wooden giants. I can see patches of red through the thick black clouds and I only see them through patches in the canopy of branches. My half Worm-eaten soul feels calmer under the shelter of the trees. Though they are slowly either dying or mutating from the new bloody crimson sky above they still anchor me to the time before the Worms. When there was green, and life, and people every-fucking-where. Before I allow my mind to drift back and fully rip open the memory scar tissue Billy just tickled, I hear music. Wild, chaotic, yet groovy enough I begin bobbing my head.

It rings through the trees, terrible and lovely, muffling my other senses. In the back of my mind I hear Billy and Lila arguing. Lila is having a wicked craving fit, while mine is somewhat subdued between the serene trees and frenzied music. Her fit is butting heads with Billy's Worm-chewed thought process. Focus blurry, I stumble forward away from the quarreling duo following the erratic beats through the trees.

I realize Billy brought us to the park as I stare out from the tree line. Weeks of abandonment have left the grass to grow wild in the poisoned sunlight. Nature adapts, however, and deep purple veins infect every blade of grass, tiny waving green and violet fingers beckoning me towards the blissfully chaotic sounds. Waving blades tickle the calloused sides of my feet over the edge of my flip-flop. The stage formally used for high school musicals, talent shows, charity auctions, and other city park bullshit is now barricaded with a hodge-podge of picnic benches and trash cans. In between the legs of up-turned tables I see the shadows of the music makers moving behind the make-shift barricade.

I notice the area surrounding the stage littered with corpses in various states of decay half obscured by the over grown two toned grass. Then, I notice two girls (one blonde and one brunette) in skimpy jean shorts with bright colored patches and worn neon pink tee-shirts burst from the tree line next to the stage. The blonde one carries a large bright orange and green quilt; the brunette carries a bright plaid case I immediately recognize as a Worm-kit. I care not for whom these girls are, where they came from, or anything else about them but I'm ready to kill them both for what's in their kit. My dry mouth begins to salivate with an acidic drool as they remove their clothes and toss them in a pile next to the blanket. They embrace passionately, running finger tips up and down each other's bodies exploring valleys and canyons, and the music seems to warp into a quicker, more off-kilter beat. The girls crumble to the ground with tongues and limbs entwined.

I'm planning their murders as I whisper-shout back to Lila and Billy. "Lila! Billy!"

They can't hear me over their incessant bickering so I back up from the tree line, careful to keep the naked women (and more importantly their Worm-kit) in my line of site, to shout a little louder over their nonsensical argument.

"Well, o' course, me crew 'ad some purse but dem Immunies kilt dem all an' den burnt da fuckin' buildin' down justa make sure dey're dead." Billy waves his sock-puppet hand in the air and shouts at Lila with her thin arms folded across her chest.

"And where the fuck is your personal, Billy Shanks?" Lila snaps as if she has snapped it a dozen times already.

He holds his hands to his mouth and uses them like a bull horn, "Me purse isn't 'ere!"

"Where is it?" Lila snarls.

"I'll tell yeh, but yeh 'ave to help me out." Billy communicates with his bobbing sock fist before crossing his arms across his turquoise adorned chest and nodding at me.

"I'm not an assassin Billy." I answer, then, quick to use their attention, "There are two weaponless girls, striped down and ready to slam some Worms. Right now. By the stage."

"Nah, forget about dem den, Billyshanks, da Bastards have already got them in da sights." Billy answers, then, taking full advantage of my attention, "And yeh sure kill a lotta' folks fer not bein' an assassin."

Lila's eyes dance with the murderous sheen I feel gleaming over mine as she storms past Billy, his arms still folded across his chest. "Fuck you, Billy, we can just kill these little bitches, and you can do your own damn dirty work. Whatever the hell it is." She huffs as she reaches the tree line.

"I'm tellin' yeh. Da Bastards are gonna kill 'em first. And yeh, if yeh try fer dat stash." Billy says as his stomps over to us.

The blonde is poking her needle into a small glass jar. After a few missed attempts she draws a glowing Worm into the over-sized needle. Her brunette companion leans down, spreads her legs and buries her face in the blonde's pubis. The blonde moans and readies to shoot up into her arm as she approaches the climax her lover's tongue urges. She draws the needle back, bites her lip in ecstasy, but before she can sink the tip of the needle into her pale flesh a rifle shot rings out over the park. Her head explodes into a thick crimson mist unbeknownst to her lover, who misinterprets her death twitches as twinges of ecstasy causing her to lap at the blonde's pussy lips all the more feverishly.

Lila loosens a groan of disgust, while gales of uproarious laughter boom from the stage in response of the inadvertent oral necrophilia. The music stops and the laughter booms in the natural amphitheater and the brunette looks up from her task and commences screaming unintelligible curse words until a second shot blows her brains out of her forehead and splatters them across the porcelain colored skin of her lover. The body falls back between the other's legs as if to return to her final act. Another peel of obnoxious laughter echoes through the park with enough force the three of us visibly shiver.

"See, Billyshanks?" Billy voice is sober and quiet. "People call 'em da Bastards and dey've earned da moniker eight times ov'r."

A small hunched form in green sweats with a vivid red headband creeps from the shadows behind the stage and approaches the dead women in looping animalistic strides.

"Dey draw folk in wit da music, something from an Australian one man band," Billy explains, "den once dey see Worms, an' only when dey see Worms, dey fuckin' snipe dem off."

"Why do they wait to see Worms, if they are gonna kill them either way?" Lila whispers.

"Dey ain't dumb. Dey savin' on ammo, not cashin' none in unless dey getting' Worms in return," Billy explains.

The man in the green sweatsuit reaches the two fresh corpses and grabs the kit and jar in one hand and the loaded needle with the other before scampering back towards the shadowed rear of the stage.

"How many of them are back there Billy?" I ask, my murderous need ravaging my throat and making the words harsh and dry.

Billy shrugs and opens his mouth to answer but a third shot rings out interrupting him. The bullet hits the man in the green sweatsuit in his thigh. Scraps of shredded green fabric fall away from a gushing mound of a wound as the hunched man does an awkward somersault and lands in a painful looking heap. The belligerent mirth rings out again.

"One less dan I don't know." Billy answers in the ringing silence after the gunshot.

"We have that gun you stole." Lila nudges me.

"Ah, Billyshanks, dey 'ave more goons…" Billy's wide bloodshot eyes are still focused on the man in the green sweatsuit. He has sat up and is digging his fingers into his wound. He pulls his fingers back and bellows at the spurts that follow their retrieval.

"Anyways, we best get goin'." Billy urges. The scene before us holds us momentarily rapt and we ignore him.

The man in the green sweatsuit, still bellowing and bawling, clutches the ready needle and smears his blood all over it as his other hand lifts his shirt. More laughter. Another gunshot. The man's hand lies next to him still clutching the blood caked needle. The man in the green sweatsuit howls in confused agony. Another man, in a vibrant purple sweatsuit and matching purple head band, struts confidently from the shadows to the man in the green sweatsuit.

The man in the purple sweatsuit kneels down and picks up the severed hand. He removes each finger from the needle one at a time before tucking the loaded needle into the kit alongside the Worm-jar. He tucks the kit under his arm as if it was the Sunday paper and pats the man in the green sweatsuit across his face with his own severed hand. The man in the purple sweatsuit drops the hand, stands and turns around whistling the tune that I recognize when the music resumes a second later.

Another shot rings out, but the strangely erratically soothing beats muffle it considerably. The man in the purple sweatsuit doesn't flinch or slow his step. Another hole is punched in the man in the green sweatsuit and he flops in response. Another gun shot and another hole punched.

"It'll get old." Billy says and nods back to the woods. "Let's converse, Billyshanks, dey won't mess with us back 'ere in da trees."

The music isn't any easier to ignore but I follow to hear what it's going to take to get a God damned Worm in my veins.

CHAPTER TWELVE

BILLY IS CRAVING VENGEANCE LIKE WE ARE CRAVING WORMS.

I can see it in his clenching and unclenching fist and the way he keeps popping his neck as if the need for revenge is a physical weight on his shoulders. He holds the sock-puppet hand up and wobbles it so all the googly eyes tremble at us. We see our pathetic reflections in the lenses of Billy's goggles above his silently moving lips.

"De Temple," He finally starts in a quick whisper soft enough Lila and I both lean in closer to him, "'as ta be dealt wit."

Lila and I both laugh at the scope of Billy's delusion. He looks at both of us in turn, casting our reflections back at us. Of course seeing my reflection makes me feel guilty and abused so I turn my vision away the best I can.

The Temple for The Church of the Dying Star downtown is one of the largest (last documented) in the world and as such has an army of lethal Worm-strung priests and bishops and devotees. Five city blocks between the former St. Augustine Roman Catholic church and the former minor league baseball stadium have all be claimed and developed by The Church of the Dying Star. They are highly organized for a cult of Worm-junkies, having a hierarchy which mocks the traditions of ancient religions, and includes a high priest, a cardinal, bishops and deacons. The common men and women worshippers are known as Starries, and they are commonly strung out with devotion and quick to kill. They all act as brutally devoted sentries around the entire perimeter. What transpires behind the walls is mostly unknown to us heathen non-believers but as quickly as the settlement is expanding great gears of some fashion must be turning.

Lila would giggle if the craving wasn't stabbing at her, "Billy, if you want to go on a suicide run we'll trade you the machine gun for the location of your damned stash."

"Hell of a deal." I offer my opinion.

"Damn'd if it ain't, but dat ain't de proper score." Billy waves the sock puppet expressively though his face is slowly draining of color as he continues. "Yeh ain't gonna be findin' none Diggers at de graveyard. Dey all dead. Or hidin'. Dat's I sayin. Dat...Dat...I say, dat...Dat..."

Billy holds his sock puppet arm up and the other out for balance he struggles to maintain. When he got excited his Worm chewed brain tried to produce adrenaline but instead fires a weak neurological signal that crackles weakly against decaying receptors. His thoughts disintegrate. Sometimes you can bring people back from stall ups like this one and other there is no coming back, and only the slow drooling death awaits them.

Lila's cold black and white eyes meet my own and roll in unison with mine. We take a step back in case Billy just went end-blank, and might suffer any final death twitches which for a Worm- ravaged minds such twitches could be lethally violent. But, we couldn't just leave him as he was our closest route to Worms, so I line him up down the stock of the rifle and Lila squints at him down the hand gun's barrel as well. Luckily for all of us, Billy shook off his mental stutter with little worse after-effects than a dazed look on his face and string of sliver drool hanging from his bottom lip. Just to be safe we keep the weapons pointed at him.

Sweat leaks from Billy's pale forehead, and he reaches his hand (without the sock-puppet) up to remove his goggles (a first since I've known him). The music from the murderous Bastard's stronghold at the park is interrupted with echoing cracks of rifle fire. We all jump at the sound, our synchronized alarm getting us all back to focus. Without noticing him putting them back on, or ever recalling seeing Billy's eyes, his goggles are back on.

"Yeh tink' I've always had dis 'air? Dis soul-stones and tattoos? I had a family once, yeh Billyshanks. And when dey Church took over dem blocks dey barricaded thousands of people in wit' a temple all 'round us. Some of us, got on the Worms…and some of us…" Billy chokes down a lump of something that looks sour. "And some of us got stuck wit' families suddenly hook'd on Worms…and dey mostly been sacrificed by dey High Priest named Jones. I made it out, and was doin' well enough as a Wormer, but den de Church kilt almost ev'ryone I 'ad left in dis fuck'd up world. Them clunky robo-cops chasin' yeh, kilt all the rest. 'Cept fer yeh…an' Dirty Josh an' Larry Boots and 'is woman…but dat's it, ev'y body else is dead! I guess, I'm sayin' I wanna kill dem all."

Maybe it is the Worm craving clawing around in my stomach, maybe it is some forgotten sense of empathy or desperate sense of friendship or some other bullshit, but (much to Lila's obvious discontent) I offer, "Well, if it means Worms in the end, I'm down."

"You crazy fucks." Lila snarls at us.

"What yeh got ta live fer anyways?" Billy snaps back.

The feeling in the air is too tense, too honest, suffocating us in unison like a communal panic attack. I get the clearest mental image I've had sober in over four weeks, that of Lila shooting Billy in his goggles, and I speak again, calmer than either of my companions, "I've even got a way to get more guns."

CHAPTER THIRTEEN

THEY TURN ON ME, SCOWLS DRAWN TIGHT, A SHIMMER DANCING ACROSS LILA'S EYES.

I can imagine behind the lens of Billy's goggles as well.

The music clangs and throbs behind us and does nothing to alleviate the tension smothering our small group. I hold my hands up in a pleading manner; they both draw nearer to hear my gravelly voice.

"We'll just take their guns." I jerk my thumb at the fortified amphitheater once I have their full attention.

"Ah, Billyshanks, yeh said yeh had a plan!"

"I don't get it, babe. Are you fucking with me or Billy?" Lila tilts her head like a confused dog. I can't help but take offense.

"They don't kill the people until they see their Worms, right?"

With her head still tilted to the side like a mocking jerk, the smugness melts away from Lila's face. Billy nods, and makes no attempt to hide his grin.

"And we got no Worms for them to see!" Billy almost squeals.

"You two are idiots." The smugness returns mudpack thick. "Just because we have no Worms, you think those crazy murders will let us walk right up and take their guns? You are both Worm-chewed."

"Not all of us need to sneak up there," I take a deep breath, tasting air greasy with soot from the endless fires, "After all, we only have the two guns. And the handgun only has one or two more bullets. So just I'll go."

"Baby, I can't just hide back here in the woods while you go on some crazy kill mission. Especially with this creepo."

"You are damn right baby." I am quick to correct, and quick to explain, "Ain't nobody sitting here waiting for me. Billy is going to sneak about half way around with me until he gets a nice clear shot at their little bell tower. You'll be distracting them. I'll get as close as I can without being seen and hit them blitzkrieg style. Billy will pick of any snipers from above and you'll have time to get clear of the blood bath."

My long winded explanation dries out my throat and lips. Christ, I need a Worm. My adrenaline begins to flutter. Anticipation, tinged with a taste of decay a shade greener than the Worm craving begins to tickle up the back of my neck.

"What are you expecting me to do? How the hell am I going to distract them?"

She almost shrieks at me, but she chokes it back. Her reaction leads me to believe my eyes shimmered. I am feeling murderous but I can aim my rage far better than the average Wormer, and my targets have already been chosen. However, Lila doesn't know as much. So I smile and tell her, "Just dance, baby."

The music in the clearing stops. Silence hums angry and uncomfortable.

Deep within the confines of the makeshift citadel someone begins whooping and hooting. Others join in, a half dozen or so of different timbres and tones and pitches. The music throbs and clangs back to life. I kiss Lila on her sweatened forehead and head off just behind the tree line. Billy follows behind me, giggling and weeping in rotating fits.

I feel her eyes burning into my back and I have to turn around and give her a reassuring wink and smile. As fake as they feel I can't believe they offer real relief or encouragement, but it still gives her the push she needs to get in the game. To her credit she enters with grand style, swaying to the discordant beats. In a strange stroke of the luck the new song seems to contain some embryonic sense of hip-hop complete with disembodied raps from a voice I find both cultured and slang.

Lila does some jerky mockery of a belly dance, swaying her emaciated hips with her arms waving above her. But the guns remain silent. Billy and I move cautiously through the trees. I do my best to keep us in the shadows rather than casting flashes of our own shadows out for twitching eyes to spot from above. I don't wager a look out at Lila and her distracting dance until I feel the curve of the large clearing. A few feet further and I have a perfect view of the crow's nest of their little fort. I can even see the man with a neon orange bandanna covering the portion of his face not already hidden behind elaborate night vision goggles sitting hunched within.

I also have a great view of Lila. She tussles her hair and bucks her hips. She rubs her hands down from her head, over her face, stopping momentarily on her pert little breasts, before continuing down her flat abdomen with the tenderness of a mosh pit.

"Be good 'nuff spot fer mah, Billyshanks." I want to argue with Billy, but I can't. It is a damn good spot. I have to continue on. I do give Lila much more attention, her dance a car crash kind of sexy I can't keep my eye off.

I reach the rear of the fort before she takes off her top. They restart the song for her. She thanks them by giving her stiff nipples a few firm tugs and twists. She tussles her hair and bucks her hips. Her dance is looping back into a familiar pattern which seems to have the infamous Bastards distracted as shit. If they weren't they are when she undoes her button fly and lets her patch-work pants slip to the ground. She wastes no time incorporating a little rough pussy-play into her strange and awkward dance routine. She slaps at her sex, slipping fingers in and out in twos and threes and tugging on her hard slippery clit while banging her head like 80's thrash metal gods. She falls to her knees, howling and bucking like a demon on fire. Taking my eyes off of her is very difficult, and I feel drawn to her like the Beast to Bethlehem.

I take a look back at Billy and the motherfucker is beating off with his sock puppet hand in the shadows of an oak tree. I look up into the bell tower Billy is supposed to be watching and the asshole in there is jerking off too, his night vision goggles swaying franticly as he rocks back and forth. I take this as sign enough everyone is sufficiently distracted.

I stroll directly up to the side of the building, crossing the frightful grassy expanse with my eyes wanting to examine the numerous blood and gore stains I trod through but remaining diligently focused ahead. No shots ring out and my view of my masturbating girlfriend improves. She is crawling on the grass on three limbs, two knees and her left hand, while her thirds remains attentive to her burning desire.

I sneak to the front of the stage, unhindered. A quick peek through the tangle of picnic tables and garbage cans and I see two men jerking each other off while peeking out nearby holes in the clutter. I replace my eyes with the barrel of the machine gun and repress the stiff trigger. The screams are immediate and far more numerous than I could have ever imagined.

Through the deafening ring in my ears I hear Billy yelling at me. I turn around just in time to see him raise his pistol, dick still flopping free, and fire the last two bullets into the bell tower. His success is proven as the sniper slips up and out face-first, flinging his high powered rifle out as a prize as he falls to the ground in front of the fort. I slink along the front of the stage letting bursts of fire in any small opening I can find. One of these random bursts cuts the sound and releases a furious ringing silence in my ears which rattles my soul.

I reach the far end of the stage just as a small door several feet away bursts open and the man in the purple sweatsuit spills out. His spurting blood is a vibrant crimson and his hands wear slick gloves of the same color but as it soaks into his sweatsuit it turns the brilliant purple a grave rot brown. He sprawls out across the grass, using the AK-47 wrapped in neon orange duct tape he has with him as a crutch/walking stick. I kick his balance out from under him and immediately feel like a school yard bully when he falls, hard, face-first into the grass. He rolls over to face me, and tests my mettle with a staring contest.

He expects me to quiver. He expects shock. He expects mercy.

His left cheek is a gaping black crater of shredded skin and blackened tissue. I can see the remains of his bullet shattered teeth like evil geometric sculptures half-buried in ruined flesh and muscle. The tip of his nose has been sheared away leaving two gaping nostrils caked with deep black blood-boogers. His eyes are wide and wild, the rainbow sheen of homicidal urges glowing like a wounded camp fire.

I aim my machine gun at his right cheek. He snarls at me, mutilated demonic, and blood seeps from his face wound and his ears. I suppress the trigger and a quick series of loud empty clicks answers back.

The man in the purple sweatsuit cackles through his ruined mouth, and it echoes wetly out his shredded cheek-flesh. I realize I really have no mercy left, and his death will not be as quick as a strong twitch and loud bang. I hold my arms out to my side, letting the machine gun slip slowly from my hands. The man in the purple sweatsuit, perhaps interpreting my stretch as me allowing him a chance at survival, scrambles to retrieve the AK I kicked six feet away. Before I can react, Lila grabs the drooping gun and stomps past me.

She steps on the man in the purple sweatsuit's hand as he reaches for the AK he has worked so hard for. She digs her heel in and grinds into the top of his hand, wet cracking sounds pop in the air around me. His screams are twice as frightening when they echo through his hollow cheek. She removes her foot, slowly and deliberately, and once free the man rolls to his back and clutches his broken hand to his chest.

His grimace is horrid, twice as much so once Lila smashes the butt of the machine gun at the bridge of his destroyed nose. She releases whatever sexual-aggressive tensions she is being tormented by as she smashes his wailing head to a crunchy pulp.

She keeps going long after he is dead. I lose interest and pick up his AK. It is fully sighted in, considerably well-cleaned, carrying a full clip of ammunition and has the word MOLLY scrawled across the layer of neon orange duct tape wrapping it. I like it. I even find two more clips of ammo tucked into the front of the man in the purple sweatsuit's sweat pants before he shits himself one last time.

I like my new toy, my killer MOLLY.

CHAPTER FOURTEEN

THE AIR IS MOIST WITH THE SMELL OF BLOOD.

Red rivers run under the makeshift barricade on the stage, drizzling over the edge in a hundred places to soak into the mud below. In the resounding silence of music and gunfire I can hear it all run over and through the planks of the stage. I see it running down the stairs the man in the purple sweatsuit fell down, but can hear it dripping and splashing and pooling as if my ears are only tuned to blood.

Lila's naked torso is speckled in brilliant crimson blood splatter, small shards of skull, and larger wet chunks of brain. She is taking deep breaths, her thin chest heaving. Her nipples, sticky with the gore of the man she just murdered, are still stiff. She catches my lingering eyes and smiles at me.

"How'd ya like my dance, baby?"

I open my mouth to answer but Billy reaches us in a celebratory mood. He hands Lila a tangled knot of her shed clothes, which she takes, without breaking eye contact with me. He closes the gap between us with his body and wraps his arms around us. He laughs directly into ears, and like that my blood drain symphony is drown out under his mirth.

"Yeh heathen Billyshanks are savage and sexy! I'll drag 'um out, yeh pat 'um down fer Worms and goons."

He kisses me on the cheek with his surprisingly soft lips. "Sexy shootin', Billyshanks."

Billy turns his head and kisses Lila on her cheek with the same brevity, and tells her "Sexy dancin', Billyshanks."

Within seconds he bounds up the blood-slick stairs and disappears into the slaughter filled darkness. In under a minute he is dragging out a man in a blood soaked yellow sweatsuit and dumping him on the grass next to us. Billy slaps his hands together, flinging the dead man's blood all over, and turns back to his chore with a smile. The Immunie gun punched a cluster of fist-sized holes into the man's ample bowel tract. His half-digested feces bubble out of his terrible wounds, and I can't help but notice the glowing neon streaks in the pasty green black muck.

Lila looks at the messy wound and dry heaves. I give her the time she needs to compose herself.

"You can have next," I say.

She smiles appreciatively, wipes at the gore drying on her chest a few times and steps into her patchwork pants. She has her tee shirt over her head when Billy drags out the next corpse. He lays the carcass of a rail-thin woman held together with only a few rough bits of sinew and strained muscle at her feet, and dashes back inside before she sees him like some foul-humored corpse-fairy.

Lila reacts less-than enthusiastically to his morbid gift, but sits down next to me and my corpse. She digs right into the slop, surged with energy of the chance of finding a Worm we so badly need. I find no Worms on the man with the exploded bowel, only a .38 snub-nose in a sweat stained ankle holster. I unfasten it from his bloated ankle and toss it next to me just in time, because Billy has me another corpse to frisk this one faceless and clad in a sky blue sweatsuit. Lila uses a hair-tie she takes off her first corpse's wrist to tie her black hair back out of her face as Billy brings her another.

Billy moves like a tireless machine steadily dragging out corpses and guns from the stage. He stacks all the guns he finds in a pile by the door, and drags the bodies to me or Lila. We search them, finding all manner of professional and homemade weapons, and then stack them in a rough half circle pile. Billy is moving so quickly he doesn't notice all the twitching when he drops me off a body which isn't quite dead. He is already halfway up the small stair case before he turns back around at my voice.

"Uh, Billy, we got a live one." I point down at the man in the orange sweatsuit at my feet gasping for breath through a throat wound which whistles with his breathing effort. The man's wide frantic eyes focus on me so I assume he knows what is happening around him. His hands and feet are twitching and he makes so effort to crawl away, so I assume he has suffered some nerve damage to go with his breathing impediment. Billy looks at the body he just dropped off and shrugs as he walks back down the stairs.

As Billy reaches us, I ask the man in the orange sweatsuit if he has any Worms. He does his best to spit at me but the action proves excruciating and the worst I get is a furious grimace. Billy grabs a random instrument of death from the stack we've found on the dead, a seven inch blade with neon nail-polish Worms painted on the handle, and crams it under the man in the orange sweatsuit's jaw opposite his previous wound. The angry eyes cloud and blink glossy. Billy pulls the knife back out with a whispery squish and lets the head drop.

I hear voices; distant, unintelligible. I look at Billy and Lila and they are looking around as if they hear the phantom voices as well. With our location smack in the middle of the grassy park completely surrounded on all sides by a dense ring of woodlands the voices sound like they are originating from everywhere. Distant shrieks of laughter and howls of torment join in the growing cavalcade of sound.

"Much left inside, Billy?" My voice is firmer than I intend but the sounds around me are making me nervous.

"Dey been 'ere since the beginnin'." He waves his sock-puppet hand at the corpses he has dragged out for us to pillage. "I got all dey bodies. I ain't found no Worms, but dey got lots o' places to stash Worms, Billyshanks. And goons and bullets e'vrywhere."

As Billy chatters away, my mind unravels. Even though I've spent the past hour or so rolling the bodies over and checking them head to toe for weapons or Worms my mind had detached from the fact I killed these people. Well, most of them. And, though we've got a shit load of guns and ammo, it doesn't look like we'll be getting any Worms from this slaughter.

And we've got too many guns for the three of us to tote them away. All of this and I see the first set of glowing eyes reach the tree line.

I hear Billy asking me questions, but his voice is muffled under my oceans of thought. He gives up, and bounces back inside without noticing all the Wormers gathering around the park. I count six or seven sets of eyes glimmering with murderous intent. Luckily most of them seem to be clustering together and none have left the shadows of the trees. Lila finally finishes with her last corpse, and wipes her hands clean on its pink sweatsuit.

She notices the eyes as she stands up. "Baby?"

"I see them. I think it is time to leave."

I'm already picking through the pile of homemade shivs for a few easy to carry ones. Lila kneels down next to me and does the same. Billy leaps off the steps with a huge empty black duffle bag in each hand.

"We's got company, Billyshanks." Billy says without looking at the massing eyes, easily over twenty people now stalking through the forest where we can see them.

"We see 'em too, Billy." Lila informs him.

"Huh?" Billy looks up, scans the tree line and the Wormers now emerging from the trees, "Oh, yeh got get movin' ifn' we don''t want 'nother fight. But I'm talkin' about dey vehicles I be hearin'."

"Huh?" It must be my turn to be surprised. I try to listen for the sound of distant engines but with the Wormers yipping and laughing as they slink from the shadows and the steady pounding of my heart in my ears I am rendered functionally deaf. I decide not to stand on circumstance and quickly help Billy stuff the duffle bags as full of guns and matching ammo as possible. Lila is there to help us get the heavy bags over our shoulders just as the first of the Wormers reach us.

He is a mess, wearing shit and piss stained jeans and a sweat and cum stained shirt with a horrible cartoon rendering of a panda with the word 'Boss' above it in different neon balloon letters. He wears no shoes, but I doubt he can even manage sandals with all the infected track marks dotting the top of his dirt-caked feet and connected with veins of dark blue infection just under his pale skin. His hair hangs in wild clumps, and his sunken cheeks are covered in an oddly patchy beard. His right arm tremors at his side, slapping inadvertently at his thigh as he struggles to control it. He shouts when he confronts us.

"Any Worms?" He gives us all personal distrustful glares, while his trembling hand, scratches randomly at his chest and stomach under the goofy shirt.

"Nah, but take what yeh want." Billy says nodding at the few guns we left scattered about the ground.

The man follows Billy's gesture slowly until his dazed eyes fall upon the remaining guns. He dives down and grabs a solid black 12 gauge shotgun. He jumps back up to his feet cackling dryly as a few other Wormers shuffle forward urged by his bravado. He spins on his heels and points the gun, which we both know to be empty, directly at us.

"Give us your Worms, mother fuckers!"

Even above his squealed demand I finally hear the engines Billy had been talking about. And it sounds like a damned motorcade headed this way.

"We told you once, shit-bag, we have no Worms. And we don't have time to play this shit with you right now." I hand MOLLY to Lila, who immediately aims it at the approaching mob of Wormers. I feel for one of the two knives I added to my leather belt. I'm going to kill this asshole.

"I'm not playing, asshole!" To prove his point, he gives the empty chamber a useless pump and points it at my crotch. "Give us your Worms or I'll blow your goddamn balls off!"

The crowd of twitching junkies behind him feeds on the chaos and cheers their man on. They don't notice the first of the vans rolling down the overgrown road on the other side of the park. I break eye contact with the man with the useless gun and have quick silent-conversations with Lila and Billy involving only a few nods. They nod their understanding back.

"Fuck you." I tell the Wormer. I watch his rotten grin warp into a baleful scowl.

Before he has time to react, Billy points at the approaching caravan and screams, 'The Church!', at the top of his lungs. The crowd behind the Wormer turns and looks at the vans, a ripple of panic rolling through their ranks. The Wormer with the shotgun keeps his attention on me. He dry-fires the gun at my crotch. I smile at him, and slash my new tonto blade across his Adam's apple.

A total of three vans are visible in the distance now, with the steady roar of more behind them. The grassy park is filled with over three dozen Wormers gathered like zombies to flesh at the silence of the Bastard's siren music. The crowd begins panicking as their brave leader sinks to his knobby knees, his lifeblood sticking his ridiculous shirt to his scrawny chest. Lila shoves the dying man backwards and leads us through the confused frightened mob, using her pointy elbows, and MOLLY's orange tape covered butt, to form our path. The number of Wormers in the park continues to grow as does the level of panic at the caravan of vans, which is still entering the park as we escape to the tree line.

If you stay with this game long enough, the worm is bound to turn. —Hayden Fry

CHAPTER FIFTEEN

WE MAKE IT TO THE TREES WITHOUT ANY FURTHER DEATH.

But we did have to shove a few of the blank-faced Worm-chewed aside to get to there. Once in the cool safety of the trees, we hike halfway around the park in the woods before our curiosity overwhelms us. We drop the heavy bags from our shoulders and turn our attention back into the park.

A total of seven vans, six white and one black, are lined up in front of the stage and surrounded by curious and desperate Wormers. All at once the vans turn off their engines. In the next instant, they are honking horns which high-pitched and voluminous like air horns. The three of us and the mass of Wormers inside the park all cover our ears at the terrible sound. We all hear a man nearby shout in surprised agony. Lila finds him first and points out the Immunie in a tree only a few feet in front of us with his hands over his ears. We do our best to have one eye on him and one eye on the park he is watching too.

The horns cease and the vans have emptied of passengers, and are now surrounded my men and women in neon kimonos and neon masks. Every kimono has a symbol on its back of a sun half blackened out. Each of them is carrying one of two types of strange weapons; a staff with an odd half-moon blade at one end or a black baton about a foot and a half long and two inches in diameter. A squad of seven men in neon colored coveralls march through the Wormers to the stage, each man packing his own MP5 and wearing a mask representing a different animal; goat, rat, cobra, horse, bear, lion, and hog. They wear the same black sun on their backs despite the variety of neon colors in their coveralls. 'Deacons' Billy informs me with a whisper. Three men stand on the black van, each in a long flowing robe of a different neon color- pink, orange, and yellow, each with a tall sharp pointy hood. Billy identifies them as Bishops. The Bishop robes all have the same dying sun symbol, each in a different neon color than their robe.

We hear the Immunie in the tree speak into a microphone on his headset. "I have visual confirmation of Bishop Quinto, Bishop Denton, and Bishop Waldrop. Yes, sir, I will record visual confirmation." After a pause: "No sir, no visual confirmation on Cardinal Ray or High Priest Jones." Another pause, during which I faintly hear Mafint's unmistakable whine, "No, sir, I lost visual on the three who initiated the slaughter, they looped around the stage. Yes sir, I will remain vigilant, sir."

I look to Lila and she mouths the word 'shit' dramatically. I nod in response. Billy gives us a deformed looking thumbs-up using his sock-puppet hand.

Back in the clearing, the man in the orange robe- Bishop Denton speaks to the still gathering crowd in a charismatic baritone. "Good afternoon, brother and sisters!"

The crowd reacts to his booming voice with a mix of awe and confusion. The Church members, commonly known as Starries, bang the butts of their staffs and tridents on the ground in erratic cadence. The squad of men exits the stage lead by a man in a neon goat mask. He slowly shakes his head 'no' to the bishops. The seven man squad disperses, and one stands in front of each van; the man in the goat mask in front on the black van.

Bishop Denton winces slightly, and holds up his hands to the crowd in a sympathetic gesture. "Sadly, my new friends, I have just been informed there are no Worms left in this former stronghold."

The crowd reacts slowly, their confusion gradually turning to hollowing disappointment. And, then, to the easiest emotion for Wormers to manifest: anger. We can hear people sobbing and shouting random curses throughout the mob. An air of unease permeates a gathering of flies to the corpses we left behind. The Bishops atop the van soak in the people's misery, making sympathetic gestures and casting understanding glances out to the crowd. The three men share a smug smile.

"However," Bishop Denton booms, "for those of us with The Church of the Dying Star there are always Worms, as the Worms are the givers of joy and mercy and joyous merciful demise! Shit, I'm high right now! Yeeeeaaah!"

His proclamation is met with a round of hoarse cheers. "How many of you here today are feeling the mercy radiating from the Dying Star? How many of you wish to rejoice in the glowing arms of The Mother Worm today? How many of you want to offer your service and lives in exchange for holy highness?"

There is a small chorus of scattered affirmatives and one man simply screaming 'Worms!'

Perhaps expecting a greater response, Bishop Denton rephrases his question, "Who wants some fucking Worms, huh?"

The crowd, sedated and irritated and confused, comes alive. Thin arms lift boney fists to pump in the air and every junkie screams for the Worms. I feel swept up in the mob mentality and have to fight the urge to run into the park to get myself a promised Worm. Billy must sense not only my urge but Lila's as he grabs our arms and nods at the Immunie in the tree only ten feet away. He tilts his head, reasoning with us silently, desperately to stay still for now. We settle into place and return our attention to the Bishops.

Bishop Denton makes no effort to raise his already loud voice, so when he speaks over the cheers and howls of the crowd he is almost drowned out in their mirth. In order to hear his instructions the crowd presses forward on the black van.

"Yes, now I got your attention didn't I?" His laughter is cold and joyless, the fruition of a dark plan. "Now, in order to reap the rewards of The Church of the Dying Star, you must serve the Church. We only have so many Worms with us, so only the most dedicated will have the opportunity to earn them." Bishop Denton holds up two fingers into the air above him, "Two things, brothers and sisters! Two acts of devotion, to earn a chance to rejoice in our mercy!" Bishop Denton holds the excited crowd rapt. He shares another wicked look with his fellow Bishops. He curls one of his fingers down, so only his pointer finger remains elevated. "The first test of your devotion, o' hopeful brothers and sisters, and the first step to getting some Worms in the needle…" He pauses long enough to draw the Wormers in like flies to a shit. From our hiding spot in the woods I see the murderous glimmer in eyes all throughout the park. Bishop Denton smiles at the shimmering hate in his crowd's eyes. "…kill the person next to you!"

CHAPTER SIXTEEN

VERY VAGUELY I REMEMBER A TIME BEFORE THE WORMS.

I can see ghosts of children playing in the park, taking full advantage of the wide open expanse of lush grass as they dart about under the summer sun. I see a spectral show on the stage, a band dressed in jeans and tee-shirts striking dramatic poses as they play their instruments with passion and intensity. The sounds of their music seems slowed and muffled, perhaps the nerves responsible for the audio portion of my memories is Worm-chewed and failing. In front of the stage I see families and young couples spread out on plain, blandly-patterned blankets. Some have picnic lunches, and others just lay on their backs soaking up the sun and atmosphere.

The scene slows, then, jerks fast, before skipping back into normal speed. The edges of my vision begin to sizzle. The band plays on. I see so many people hugging, kissing, and smiling.

I blink and it's all gone.

The grass, so lush and green in my haunted memory, is an absurd mixture of overgrown and pale. The dangerous tangle of picnic tables and garbage cans occupies the space for the band. No people remain enjoying the show on their simple blankets, replaced with the corpses of the Bastards. No children play pick-up games of baseball with ball-cap bases where dozens of Wormers crowd together listening to the words of a madman in a bright neon orange robe.

Bishop Denton's words hang in the air above the crowd, and they all stare at him for a moment as if to determine his seriousness. As the words flutter down like hateful snowflakes onto the crowd they react like the godless heathens they are. Within seconds violence has engulfed the park, everywhere we look people are attacking each other like savages. I watch a young woman giving herself a tight hug, suddenly sway back at the waist and then spring forward at the middle-aged woman next to her. The younger woman snaps her head forward as she strikes, driving her forehead into the older woman's startled face. A man wearing a yellow tank-top and leather underwear lurches forward and wraps his arms around the neck of the man in front of him. They crash to the ground and the man in the tank top wraps his legs around his victim's body to squeeze away his life two fold. A man and a woman run at each other from twenty paces, crashing together in a flailing mess of limbs which topples into another crowd of people punching and kicking at each other.

They trample over the bodies we left and each other as they fall, a violent swarm swirling around the park in a fashion my madness almost recognizes as a pattern. It doesn't take long for the scattered homicidal combatants to find the pile of shivs and shanks and the guns we couldn't carry. The battle kicks up a notch, and the blood really begins to flow. Stabs and slashes replace punching and kicking.

Apparently, the crowd of Wormers had kept the weapons hidden from the view of the Bishops and Deacons. When the first shots ring out, the Starries and the blasphemous clergy springs into action. Bishop Quinto jumps closer to the action on top of the closely parked vans, though each jump requires a short running start. His pink robe flaps in the air as he jumps and skids his way to the van nearest the gunfire. Once he reaches the van he shouts at the Hog Deacon to 'squealsh this shit.'

Hog Deacon nods at Bishop Quinto, the eyes of his hog mask bloodshot and sad, and walks around the van. As he marches around the fender he raises his MP5 and suppresses the trigger. The Deacon's shooting is most impressive, his first burst of gunfire dropping six Wormers dead, and disarming another two.

"Now, no guns, brothers and sisters," Bishop Denton shakes his head disappointedly at the bloody crowd. "You can just turn any old guns you find to one of our loyal Starries. We'll gladly let you keep those blades you have all seemed to stumble upon at once. Be warned though, The Church of the Dying Star will show no mercy to heretics and threats to our dear Church."

As if to punctuate his leader's message, Hog Deacon lets loose two more bursts at the Wormers cluttered around the stray guns. The second burst is aimed low and sweeps back and forth in a far wider arc than the first burst. I doubt any of the eight who fall are dead, but they ain't ever dancing again. The third burst is at head level and claims two exploding skulls as rewards.

After the last spent shell drops silently to the grass, Bear Deacon leads the Starries surrounding the third van with him to meet with Hog Deacon and his squad. Once the two units join those holding the black batons, they give them a firm twist about mid-way and a blade nearly the length of the baton slides out one end. I'm slightly shocked to see nearly as many women as men, but they all step forward as one. Those with the bladed staffs put them to use hacking away at those Wormers unfortunate enough to fall to Hog Deacon's bullets. The Starries with the baton swords retrieve the cache of guns from the Wormers, resulting in several more Wormer deaths and not a single other shot fired.

Bear Deacon is walking a slow circle around the carnage, surveying the ground for any more unclaimed guns. He spots something under the mutilated corpse of a red-haired Wormer. He kneels to get a better look and then calls a Starry over to him. He points the gun he spies to woman and she goes about crawling through the blood to retrieve the weapon for him.

Bear Deacon is watching her and nodding slightly as a Wormer whirls out of a crowd behind him with eyes glimmering the familiar hateful rainbow. The Wormer flails his slender arms wildly as he leaps at Bear Deacon's back. His thin arm wraps around the Deacon's neck and jerks his head back. The Wormer's other hand is tightly clutching a neon green lock blade pocket knife he stabs wildly at Bear Deacon's face with. The thin sliver of metal punctures the papier-mâché bear mask and sinks into Bear Deacon's cheek. Before anyone can react, the Wormer jerks his blade back and stabs into the mask another five times, each more vicious than the last. The nose of the bear mask is crushed during the frenzied attack and the torn papier-mâché soaks in a great deal of the blood gushing from Bear Deacon's wounded face.

Goat Deacon runs from his position by the black van and Horse Deacon shifts over from the next closest van and to assume his spot. The Wormer attacking the Bear Deacon is still smiling wildly, and Bear Deacon's struggles are growing weaker. Goat Deacon opens fire from thirty feet away and walks straight towards the men. His MP5 blasts through Bear Deacon's broad chest and into the frail desperate Wormer behind it. By the time Goat Deacon is standing above his targets the resulting mess is torn to shreds and swamping blood into the grass.

Away from the skirmish over the guns the ultra-violence is all over the park. With the help of Hog Deacon's kills, the number of living Wormers in the park is quickly reduced by half. The Starries all leave their posts by the vans, walking in pairs to the nearest loser, be they dead or dying. The Starries armed with swords stab them through the heart and then the staff-bearers raise their weapons in the air before bringing them down and decapitating the body. Each pair performs the same ritual, then moves on to another.

Bishop Denton stomps his foot on the roof of the black van and claps his hands with furious devotion. The surviving Wormers are drawn to him, and stagger over the dead and dying to reach the celebrating man in the flowing bright orange robe.

"Well done, brothers and sister!" The three Bishops shout repeatedly at the survivors.

Bishop Denton makes a big production, including the playful chugging of his arms and marching his legs like an animated choo-choo, before he raises one finger high into the air above him. "One task down, and one step closer to a Worm! Only one task of devotion left to go, my blood-baptized brothers and sisters!"

CHAPTER SEVENTEEN

BISHOP DENTON'S SECOND TASK IS LABOR INTENSIVE.

First, he orders all the heads gathered up and laid in front of the black van. He demands each head has its dead eyes cast in the direction of the gyrating Bishops. Next, he has them gather up each headless corpse and drag them all to a central pile. The Wormers work slowly under the swirling crimson sky, several collapsing with with-drawl cramps, but the Bishops are patient.

When the grisly task is finally complete, the remaining Wormers are completely drenched from head to toe in blood, gore, and post-mortem feces.

But Bishop Denton isn't finished. His next order draws incredulous stares from exhausted blood-shot eyes. "We need to wall us in now, brothers and sisters, as only a fortunate few deserve the mercy of the Church of the Dying Star." The Starries bang their staves on the ground. "Luckily, my new friends, we have a supply to quickly build such a wall!"

The crowd reacts like zombies, some not even blinking and only a few casting expecting glances to the vans.

"The stage, brothers and sisters, tear it down and re-build it as a wall for this land I now claim for The Church of the Dying Star!"

A shiver of discontent moves through the crowd. In response the animal-faced Deacons step forward and check the safety on their MP5s. I look away from the tense moment to the stack of heads. At the very top of the pile rests the Bear Deacon's head, his mask bloody and destroyed.

Regardless of their exhaustion, some Wormers drag the picnic tables to the tree line fairly evenly spaced. Others work at tearing apart the stage plank by plank, and then passing them to another group of Wormers who add the planks to a rickety fence which quickly blocks our view.

Luckily for us, the Immunie in the tree is high enough up his view is barely obscured and he is whispering to Mafint through his headset offering the cyborg detailed play-by-play. As he is ordered, the soldier records whatever is happening behind the wall.

We sit and wait for what feels like hours before we hear Mafint's terrible voice answer back. "Excellent work, Cadet Steffen, with this many of the Church hierarchy and fire power distracted with this new project the Counsel has decided to attack the main Church. Report there now, soldier!"

"Yes, sir!" Cadet Steffen barks into his headset, confident the noise of the construction drowns out his distant voice. The middle-aged man shimmies backwards out of his position, and repels down the tree in two clumsy hops. He hits the ground and unhooks all his harnesses in an obvious rush for battle.

The eager, yet flushed man, grunts as he gains his footing on aged knees. He looks up in the direction he plans on running but before he can take a step a bullet hits him dead center in his forehead and the tree he just dropped from is spackled in his brains and blood. Cadet Steffen crumbles at the base of the tree, his dead eyes staring dumbly at the smoking barrel Billy is pointing at him until he hits the dirt.

CHAPTER EIGHTEEN

WE'RE RUNNING AGAIN.

Following Billy through the trees, we were hefting a heavy-assed bag full of guns and ammo. The bag Billy carries renders his path never quite straight as he darts through the trees to the street. We come upon an old station wagon parked in between two massive cedar trunks. The vehicle is completely covered in sheets of metal, and it has a line of two foot metal spikes welded to both the front and rear bumpers. All the glass has been removed with small slits in the metal serving as means of seeing out of the homemade tank.

I must be in a daze because I don't remember Billy frisking Cadet Steffen after he blew his brains out the back of his head, but he uses a key from a key ring to open the lock securing the top sheet of metal. Billy struggles to hold the metal lid up so I toss my bag into the back seat and help him so he can toss his in as well. Next we hold it for Lila, who scampers up and in while dragging a seductive foot from my ankle to crotch bulge as she goes. Billy smiles like a fool and nods for me to jump in first. I obey, and then stand where the back seat would have been to hold the metal roof up for Billy. He climbs into the driver's seat, the only seat

Our Worm digger uses another key from his mysterious key ring to start the vehicle. It turns over and I realize in the roar of its engine my paranoia is humming. I choke down the string of questions I want to vomit at Billy. But why rock the boat? His plan seems to be working. We actually have a hell of a lot better odds than we did two hours ago. Billy smiles like he expected all of this, as he careens through the trash strewn, yet greatly abandoned streets.

"Where are we going now, Baby?" Lila asks. I assume she really knows and just wants to communicate with me to help stave off the encroaching Worm craving. It's already rotting my mood, and I don't care to humor her.

"Ask Billy," Is all I offer her.

Billy doesn't even give her time to scoff at me, though she shoots me a stink eye while he talks. "Aww, Billyshanks, we be findin' Dirty Josh an' Larry Boots and 'is woman."

Lila is persistent. "Who are these people, baby? Where do they live?"

"I really don't know, baby. I'm just along for the Worms." I try to smile at her, but it feels broken and blatant.

"Dey friends o' mine. Good people, crazy killers. Like yeh!" Billy shouts as he navigates the city streets through the small slots in the metal. "Not sure where dey be, but I get us close!"

True to his word, Billy drove us to an apartment complex about two blocks from his old graveyard. He drove our new ride into a wide empty parking lot shared by four different buildings, each five stories tall. Billy wedged the car as tight as possible in between the wall and an overflowing dumpster.

"We gonna 'ave to split up ta' save time. Each of us take a buildin' and den meet back up 'ere." Bill speaks while digging through his black bag of guns. I follow his lead and dig MOLLY out of my bag. Once I find her and rest her on my lap, I dig Lila out an MP5 which looks like it could have an animal-faced

Deacon as a previous owner. Once armed, we shimmy one by one out the roof.

Distracted, fiending and paranoid, I wander off towards the most distant building without a word to my companions. Lila finds this unacceptable.

"Baby? What the fuck?" Her tone is sharp, the MP5 tucked under her armpit as she scolds me.

I shrug. "What the fuck what?"

Lila stomps across the blacktop until she is standing right in my face. "You mad at me? You've been kind of a prick since my dance. The dance you made me do."

I hear the argument in a flash of crimson-tinted precognition. I shake it away. I don't care how she danced, I don't care if every man in the park jerked off at her while she was dancing. Who the fuck cares? I jerk my cock whenever I want to. Lila is here and here most often, but the Worms get the juices flowing and, well, monogamy becomes impossible as general self-control breaks down. Jealousy is a wasted emotion in the time of the Worms. We are all filthy, depraved killers, doing filthy, depraved things while we kill for the next high. That quiet voice of reason, the conscience, was the first thing Worms destroyed in users. Somehow, I've managed to keep a tighter grip on my mind than most. I could argue with her, we could scream and yell and fight right here in the middle of the empty parking lot, and to be honest the thought of having no Worms makes me want to smash a pretty face in, but now is not the time. Maybe after we get good and high we can fight and fuck. For now, I concede.

"I'm fiending, that's all."

"Then kiss me. And not just a little peck goodbye. Kiss me like you can't wait to eat my pussy."

She smiles wickedly and wraps her arms around my neck to pull me close. Her cold lips gently touch mine, and her tongue slithers into my open mouth. She presses past my own limp tongue to lick as deep into my throat as she can. She nearly gags me, and as I struggle against the choke she reaches up and gives my nipple a firm tweek. I feel the blood rush through my body, my vision blurs and thoughts reel as my brain swells with blood like a mushroom trip. My fingers and toes go numb, a pins-and-needles sensation dancing to my extremities. My cock, half-hard since Lila's dance in the park, pulses twice into a full erection pressing against Lila's flat stomach. Along with everything else, my tongue springs to excited life, and tangles up her tongue like a wrestler taking down an opponent.

Her knees go weak, but her arm muscles flex pulling me closer. MOLLY drops from my numb hands, before I grab Lila around her waist. I let my fingers tickle over the exposed pale flesh of her stomach, then sink just below the edge of her pants, as I slide them around to her ass cheeks. Gripping her tender ass, I squeeze her closer, yet still my dick just throbs hot and stiff between us. She moans into my mouth, and drools out the corner of her. I grab her face by her cheeks; lick the salty slobber away before licking down her smooth cool neck.

"Oi, ya randy Billyshanks!" Billy nudges us hard enough we stagger a few steps apart. We stare at him for a second and he points at us both and then the buildings we should be searching for his friends.

"Jesus, Billy, we don't even know these people, they are your fucking friends. Can't you just stand here and holler for them?" Lila speaks to Billy but doesn't take her eyes off of me, even allowing them to wander to the uncomfortable buldge left in my crotch.

"Ah," Billy waves her words away with his sock-puppet,"Dey Dirty Josh an' Larry Boots."

"Yeah, you say that like they were movie stars or something, Billy." I point out, unable to take my eyes off of Lila's pert nipples fighting the weak fabric of her tee-shirt.

"Well," Billy scratches his head with his sock-puppet hand, forcing his hair to wave wildly in the air, "Dirty Josh 'as a lot of ink an' a belly on 'im. Larry Boots is a tall of black fella with bright 'air like that crazy black basketball player…"

Lila and I share a look of utter confusion. Billy looks at it and waves us off again. "And Larry Boots 'as a woman with blonde 'air. Pretty little number. 'E calls 'er Babycakes." He gives Lila a look like a horse eyeing a salt lick. She flips him the bird. "Anyways, we best be splitting up, fer the sake o' time, Billyshanks."

I nod my understanding to Billy. Lila tilts her head, her discontent etched under her high cheek bones. I blow her a slightly obscene kiss, and use my eyes to promise a continuation of our fun. She sighs disappointedly and reaches two fingers down the front of her pants. Her forearm flexes as her fingers sink into her moistness. She draws fingers back and into her mouth. She makes an elaborate show of sucking on them before using them to blow me a kiss back.

Billy uses his sock-puppet hand to blow us both quick angry kisses.

We turn as one and stumble off to separate buildings, to search for Billy's friends. I check the safety on MOLLY as I step onto the overgrown path which leads me to the front of the apartment building.

CHAPTER NINETEEN

THERE IS THE CORPSE OF A MAN LYING OUTSIDE THE FRONT DOOR.

Its arms are splayed wide open as if it wants to hug me to its bloated chest. I notice with an odd sense of familiarity the corpse has the name 'BOB' carved across its chest. One of its shoeless feet rests on the bottom stair. Is my brain looping back on itself? I look at the corpse's face, and it bears little resemblance to the BOB where our journey started. This one has a much flatter nose and droopy bulldog cheeks. Just to be safe, I pat him down and find nothing.

I step over the corpse and its smell rises up to meet me, a silent yet fierce guardian of the apartment building. The front double doors are slightly ajar, several bloody handprints smeared across the cheap-gold plated door handles. I hear a few noises from the darkness beyond the doors, but I can't differentiate them from moans or thuds. Something tells me I'm in the right place.

The doors push open soundlessly and I creep into the lobby. I hear the noises clearer, moans and thuds- people fucking. If my ears are being fair, I'd say from up on the fourth or fifth floor. The reek of rot and decay is so strong on the ground floor I have to cover my nose with one arm while holding MOLLY out in front of me. I make a quick round through the gagging stink of the first floor and find every door shut. Still I listen at each one and hear nothing except the steady buzzing of flies.

The second floor is completely empty of any signs of life. Almost all the furniture from all four apartments is crammed into a single rear unit. Two of the others look like people have used them as crash pads for a while and then moved on leaving only scattered debris behind. The forth is completely covered in clear industrial tarp. Pictures still hang on the walls; their images blurry behind the plastic. My nerves feels raw, and I'm twitching so bad MOLLY's barrel bounces around to the point of uselessness. I leave the apartment without venturing deeper than the living room and kitchen.

I find a number of dead bodies on the third and fourth floors. Looks like a few suicides and a few ODs. Nothing out of the ordinary, and still nowhere near the reek of the first floor or the strange eeriness of the plastic covered room on the second floor. The sounds of people fornicating keeps getting louder and louder the closer to the fifth floor I get.

Once I make it up the small staircase to the fifth floor groans, moans, and grunts echo all around me, punctuated by steady hard banging. None of the doors are closed and the sounds are so loud it is impossible to tell where they are coming from. So I have to look inside of each. I find them in the third.

I knock on the frame of the open door, and as I expect I get no direct response. So, I let myself in. I step into a living room decorated with hundreds and hundreds of dangling strips of bright colored tissue paper reaching down to the cluttered floor. In the middle of the room, hardly visible through the neon jungle, I spy a naked woman bent over a couch spray painted neon green and pink. A tall thin black man with hair like an acid-trip leopard has his hands gripping tight to her slender hips as he bucks against her. I figure this to be Larry Boots. The woman, I assume his girlfriend, Babycakes, groans with his every thrust, but the cock in her mouth muffles those moans of pleasure. The white man she is sucking is nearly covered in vivid tattoos, has a solid looking pot belly, and has a knotted and filthy ponytail nearly as long as the one he is gripping on now. I deduct this fella is the one Bill calls Dirty Josh. Larry Boots slams harder and harder, in turn forcing the other man's dick deeper and deeper down Babycakes's willing throat. They pump and grind and groan, a sweat slick ecstasy machine.

I throb and think of Lila. I switch MOLLY to my left hand and let my right hand seek my own aching need as the three shift positions. Larry swings his hips backwards, allowing his eleven-inch dong to flop out and slap Babycake's ass-cheeks. He grabs her by her hip and shoulder and pulls her off of Dirty Josh's prick as he directs her to her knees. No sooner is she on the ground than the entirety of his length is in her mouth. Her cheeks bulge and her forehead sweats as she struggles to tolerate the massive penis ramming down her throat.

Larry grabs a fistful of blonde hair and forces himself forward so hard and deep Babycakes's nose smashes into his stomach. She gags and his hips buck against the choking noises. Dirty Josh shuffles around the end of the couch, stroking his member and chewing on his bottom lip, a cop-mustache hides his upper lip and aviator sunglasses hide his eyes. As he steps around his buddy, Dirty Josh gives Larry Boots a playful slap on his slim ass. Larry withdraws his huge pecker, now sufficiently covered in a thick sheen of saliva from her mouth only to hoist his ball-sack with one hand and guide her mouth under it with his other. Larry Boots hoots three times, deep and ringing and the three break into hysterics.

Babycakes jumps to her feet, her pert breasts bouncing ever so lovely as she flops back onto the couch. She spreads her legs, allowing me a peeping tom's view of her red and swollen pussy. I only get a momentary look as Dirty Josh quickly stuffs his shorter, thicker cock into the battered vagina.

At the same time Larry straddles her torso and slaps his monster in between her breasts. Babycakes squeezes her tits together, smothering his drool-slick prick in between them. The three resume their pounding and groaning; only this time I am in rhythm with them as I stroke myself from across the room. My numb feet move me forward without my conscious ordering of it until I am only five feet away from the trio, though still fairly hidden by the thickness of the streamers.

After a few minutes of grinding and grunting Larry Boots tells Babycakes, "You better get this wang all slippery with some slobber, Babycakes, cuz' I'm gonna stick it up your ass now."

"Fuck yeah, he is!" Dirty Josh chortles.

Babycakes can only gag as Larry has already filled her esophagus with big black cock. He fucks her throat as Dirty Josh pulls out and sits on the couch blocking my view of Babycakes's hammered pussy. Larry pumps violently and Babycakes's gags sound painful but Larry cheers her on with every thrust forward. Until it sounds like she pukes all over his crotch. I cease my masturbation while they reposition.

Babycakes straddles Dirty Josh and slides slowly down on his girth. She sways back and forth, working the thick cock while Larry Boots applies gentle pressure to her asshole with two fingers. He reaches one incredibly long arm to the end table and pulls back a bent and leaking tube of lubricant and squirts a liberal amount over her anticipating rectum. The next instant he is in and showing little consideration for her sphincter's integrity as Babycakes's moans take on a teary echo.

The streamers stick to my sweaty skin and obstruct my view. I avoid any further frustration and step forward all the way to the couch still fiercely stroking my cock. I stand on the opposite side of the couch, MOLLY in one hand and my dick in the other. Due to their positioning Dirty Josh is facing away from me, but both Larry Boots and Babycakes are facing me. Babycakes sees the AK47 first and I see the panic clouding in her ecstasy shimmering eyes. Larry Boots sees my hand sliding up and down my shaft and he responds with a wink. The next instant he reaches one hand forward and hooks a finger in Babycakes's mouth. He tugs her mouth open and nods at the open orifice.

I rest MOLLY against the side of the couch and let my dirty pants fall to my ankles. Babycakes notices my own impressive manhood, and is still staring wide eyed as I feed it to her. Larry Boots hoots and slams harder, sliding in and out of Babycakes's slippery asshole while Dirty Josh bucks against the weight of Larry and Babycakes pressing down on him. The harder they buck, the deeper down Babycakes's throat I go. As excited as Lila got me in the parking lot, I don't last long and soon ejaculate what feels like a quart of hot Worm-flavored jism down Babycakes's gullet. By some stroke of luck, the others reach their climaxes soon after me, none of them bothering to withdraw from which ever orifice they are stuffed into.

Babycakes wipes a clumpy trickle of my cum from her chin and asks, "Hey, what's your name?"

CHAPTER TWENTY

WORMS IN THE NEEDLE | MbS

BRIEF INTRODUCTIONS ARE MADE, BUT SEEM INSIGNIFICANT IN WAKE OF THE GROUP SEX AND ALL.

Besides I know who they are because Billy told me, and that's what I tell them as I open the window and whistle for Lila and Billy.

"Aw, good, is that crazy bastard Billy Shanks down there?" I hear the unmistakable quiver in Larry Boots' deep baritone which lets me know these three are fresh out of Worms themselves.

"He is," I don't allow people to get their hopes up when I can help it, "But he ain't holding."

Their disappointment is sharp, honing to razor-fine edge as the first nerve-scorching pangs of withdrawal greet them.

"Well, what the hell you want wit' us then?" Dirty Josh gives his half-erect penis a few strokes right in Babycakes' face. The faded Worm-high was obviously the sole source of the passion I was just allowed to share from the disgusted scowl Babycakes shoots at Dirty Josh. She cements my assumption when she balls up her tiny fist and smashes it into Dirty Josh's sagging testicles.

I can't help but wince as Dirty Josh crumples to the floor, the pain and shock in his voice evident in his cries. Babycakes scampers off the couch, and around the room collecting random scraps of clothing strewn about. Larry Boots just shakes his head and mumbles, "Damn, DJ, what ya' thinking stroking ya' ween in the girl's face?"

I clear my dry throat, their fresh withdrawal makes me jittery nervous. My sweaty palms grip MOLLY tight. I can't keep my thoughts straight enough to even attempt to explain what Billy has talked us into. I think saying it out loud in my own voice would disrupt some strange psycho-spiritual balance I've managed to bullshit myself into. "Best just to let Billy tell it."

It's all I can offer them. The cold thorny crash is ripping at them, and I don't feel safe surrounded by them in what everyone knows is a very dangerous state. "I'll send Billy up. Nice to meet you all."

None of the three look up at me. Dirty Josh is weeping, but I don't know if it's from his slugged nuts or the crash. Larry Boots is bent over the couch dry heaving. Babycakes has gotten half dressed, and is now sitting on the floor in a ratty tee-shirt with a unicorn on the front, hugging her knees and rocking back and forth.

My exit is easy, though my mind intensifies it to the point it feels like a heart-racing escape to safety. I meet Billy and Lila outside the front door, where they stand over the corpse at the small stairway. They are whispering to themselves, chummier than they typically are, and both jump a little when I stagger out. Lila blushes, a rarity, and covers her mouth with the back of her hand. I have the sudden urge to lift MOLLY and kill them both. I fight it by biting the inside of my cheek. It feels dry and fuzzy anyways, like gnawing at a fleshy yet over-ripe peach. I manage a smile at them, and feel the blood streaked across my teeth wet my dry lips as they curl up at my friends.

I win because my smile, though blood-streaked, doesn't look as nervous as theirs.

"Your friends are on the top floor, Billy."

Billy answers me with a sheepish grunt and a nod. He starts past me, an M-16 with so many bandannas tied around its barrel it looks like Steven Tyler's microphone stand flung over his shoulder.

"They are crashing right now, Billy. Be careful."

"Ya betcha', Billyshanks," He says over his shoulder as he bounds up the stairs and into the apartment building.

I turn to Lila, and she smiles at me. It is nervous, yet predatory. I shiver, and feel a trickle of sweat drip down my chest. She holds up a small hand-held camera. I tilt my head like a confused dog. She sees the blankness in my eyes, and raises her eyebrows sardonically at me. Oddly enough the mocking acts like a jolt to my brain and the memory of watching Cadet Steffen up in the tree with the same video camera plays slowly in eerie sepia-toned flashes. I watch him drop to the ground and catch a bullet to the face. I watch the tree trunk behind spatters with brain and skull bits which are soothing shades of brown, gray, and tan. I still don't see Billy frisk the corpse but we have the keys and the tankcar and the video camera so he must have. No sepia-colored flashback for it though.

This irritates me for no good reason other than I want a god damn Worm.

My eyes must shimmer. Lila looks so meek, even with the Uzi she hugs to her pert breast. Her eyes look ghost town, and her hand trembles as she offers me the video camera. I take the offered camera, and walk back in the direction of the tankcar without another word. She follows three silent steps behind me. I can hear yelling out the window I opened as we reach the parking lot and come to a sudden stop.

An armored van is parked behind the stolen tankcar. I feel my heartbeat so hard in my ears it makes me dizzy. My eyes dart back and forth between the two vehicles and I notice the lid on the tankcar is flipped up. Someone is looking inside. I spin around and shove Lila much harder than I mean to.

I prevent her from falling, but I'm afraid it isn't a particularly gentle act in itself. I usher her back way we came, stopping only long enough to see to men clad in camouflage pointing at the source of the shouting which happens to be the fifth floor.

We dart around the corner, over Bob II, and into the apartment building. I lead Lila up the first flight of stairs and then back towards the plastic covered apartment. I bang the butt of MOLLY on the wall with every step hoping those upstairs hear it and react accordingly. As we reach the plastic covered apartment, Lila rips my fingers off her wrist so hard she dislocates at least one of them. She silently refuses to enter the apartment, and I can't really blame her, but we need to hide our asses fast. We crowd into the shadows of the stairwell leading to the fourth floor as an unspoken compromise. They keep shouting above us, and soon, from our hiding place we see shadows moving around on the first floor.

I watch the shadows best I can without standing out in the hallway for them to see. Then I change my mind. Without alerting Lila to my plan, I lean MOLLY against the wall under the staircase and step slowly into the hallway. Both men are stalking silently up the stairs, looking up as they go to focus on the unintelligible voices. They don't even see me at first, so I shout to them.

"I killed Cadet Steffen. I chopped him into little bits and then put him back together. He looks just like you two now."

The Immunies aim their guns at me and tell me to hit the fucking floor. I can't see their faces behind the violet lens of their masks but I imagine they are more nervous than I am and probably can't see me as good as I can see them. I take a big risk and dash back the way I came.

They tell me to stop at the same time they fire. I duck down and to the side, while the wall to the right of me gets peppered with bullets. I slink into the shadows under the staircase before they round the small bend in the hallway. I bump into Lila, and get MOLLY's barrel jammed into my ribs. I jerk my gun out of her hands, dislocated fingers be damned. I hear the Immunies mumble something to each other as they stare through the only open door into the apartment covered in plastic. They walk past quickly, guns aimed into the apartment. The second they hit the threshold I step out of the shadows with MOLLY chest-high.

I allow them a split second to scream before I let them have it. MOLLY spits six slugs in a blistering instant. The man in front catches four and is nearly torn in half from the waist up as he falls backwards onto the other man who catches one of the two other bullets to the side of his neck. The two fall into the middle of the plastic coated living room, and I follow them right in without thinking. The first man is obviously dead and his corpse has the other, seriously wounded man pinned to the floor and draped in exploded internal organs. I check the dead man's pocket first and find the keys to their armored car. Just to be safe I grab the walkie-talkie clipped to his pocket as well.

I hear Lila shouting behind me, and the thunder of the top-floor apartment empting out as Billy and his friends come crashing down the stairs. Through the gun-shot whistle-hum deafness, I hear the second man plead with me in a wet gagging whimper. I can't hear his quiet voice well enough to tell if he is begging for life or death. I hear one more sound as I back slowly out of the apartment; the unmistakable crumpling of plastic.

I meet the others in the hallway and toss Larry Boots the keys to the new armored vehicle. Billy wants to ask questions but behind me I hear plastic crumpling and scraping and slithering and tightening. I shove past them all with MOLLY held against my chest and Lila pressed against my back.

CHAPTER TWENTY-ONE

BILLY DRIVES THE TANKCAR WE CAME IN AND LARRY BOOTS IS DRIVING THE ARMORED VAN.

We leave the parking lot as quick as possible with the promise to meet at a location both Billy and Larry Boots agree on. Lila and I bounce around in the car with no seats, so I sit down on the vibrating metal floor to check out the stolen video camera. Lila recognized Babycakes as an old flame of hers and she rambles and spits and bitches about the skinny blond but I do my best to ignore and focus on the small video screen.

The camera moves slowly over the overgrown grass, it shimmers a dead purple as it waves at the crimson sky. Impatient, I tap the fast forward button until the view tightens on a dancing Lila. The camera follows her as she bucks and crawls and sways. She strips slowly, but aggressively, and the camera begins to tremble. I am mesmerized watching Lila's slender form masturbate in the middle of that terrible park, crawling over the unnatural grass in pursuit of her groove. Yet her irate voice barking into my ear about how much of a skank Babycakes is makes my head feel like it wants to split open and spill out a demon to choke her into silence. I know she is a skank, I don't think it is the time or place to make any confessions to Lila.

On the small screen, the view darts across the expanse of the grass until it rests on me blasting into the Bastard's stronghold. My face is pale and blank, but my eyes are glowing a rainbow of strange neons. I walk slowly, deliberately across the front of the stage, blasting every few feet. As I walk around the edge of the stage I fall out of view, so the man in the purple sweatsuit's demise isn't captured on film. Instead the camera focuses on the wood of the stage and the hundreds of blood creeks flowing under the barricade and down into the dirt.

I thumb the fast forward again until the Church of the Dying Star show-up. The camera pans slow over the Starries, the animal-faced deacons, and especially on the fluorescent robe wearing bishops. I grow impatient and speed up the recording to the point Bishop Denton incites the murderous riot. When the violence broke out it was all over, too many terrible things to look at all at the same time. Cadet Steffen, the cameraman, didn't even try to capture it all. Instead he would capture slow swiping shots across the battlefield until he found something to focus his curious lens on, at which point he zoomed in as far as the camera would allow. He would remain on the fight uncomfortably long after the loser was dead, before zooming back out and scanning the random chaos until he found another brutal example of the scene.

My numb thumb presses the recording ahead again.

I watch the construction of the ramshackle wall in triple time. And I then feel blood drain from my face as I watch the remaining people in the park dig a wide open pit, forty feet wide and four or five feet deep, they drag the stacked corpses of the Bastards Billy left for them and the scattered carcasses from the slaughter to. I even see the Bear Deacon's mangled corpse before another covers it. I watch wide-eyed and pale as the survivors line up at the edge of the pit, staring down at the dead with anguish and confusion and need etched on their slender faces. The Starries surround the blood and dirt covered survivors while they are all distracted. In the next instant the Starry weapons are put to task, slaughtering the remaining people and tossing them in the hole before they realize what was happening.

Once only the Church members remain, the deacons unload a few boxes from each van and set them at the lip of the hole. The bishops retrieve jars full of glowing Worms, and I feel acidic need claw at my already raw throat. Always the thorough soldier, Cadet Steffen zoomed in on the jars unhindered by the want to leap out of his tree and murder everyone in between him and Worms. God damn the beautiful Worms, until the image sharpens into focus again and I see the mutated atrocities the man in the muumuu ate earlier. Hard sharp spines line the swollen neon Worms and I shiver visibly when the camera gets an unnerving close-up view of the circular mouths filled with tiny needle-sharp teeth at both ends of the Worms.

"What the hell is with these crazy ass new Worms, Billy?" I croak through cotton and want.

"Jus' keep peepin' it, Billyshanks." He doesn't even turn his goggles back at me.

I want more answers, but before I can argue, the bishops onscreen unscrew the lids from the jars and toss them out onto the mass grave so the jars empty of their contents as they soar through the air. The Starries bang their staffs on the ground while Cadet Steffen zooms in on the glowing Worms crawling on the corpses. Within seconds, the mutated Worms begin digging into the corpses with ravenous fury. Gore pumps from the small holes the Worms leave in the dead flesh as they burrow, and soon the bodies on top are draining their fetid contents onto those stacked beneath them. In the background of the recording I hear Mafint's high-pitched whine ordering Cadet Steffen to the massive Church of the Dying Star.

I open my mouth to ask Bill what the hell I just watched, but he answers before my words form. "Yah can't be growin' Worms in dead bodies, Billyshanks. Dey needs dirt! Grave dirt, dirt soaked with death but not dead fuckin' bodies, Billyshanks! Do ya see?"

There is a silence which feels shameful and impatient, and then Billy adds, "Dey been workin' on 'at shit for awile now."

Somehow, maybe the slightest tremble in his voice or the two quick nervous swallows he makes, but I know Billy is crying behind his goggles. Unfortunately, my curiosity presses on.

"Why, Billy? What is the point to the mutated Worms?"

"Dead bodies is cheap right now, Billyshanks. And these new Worms grow fasta'. Cheapa' and fasta', Billyshanks."

I can't restrain my scoff, "but this is the end of the world."

"Aye," Billy nods as he turns us into an alley sandwiched between to abandoned suburbanite blocks, "humans is always reckless, Billyshanks, ya think we find kindness in the heat of the comin' flames?"

Billy sees my hesitation, and pushes just a little more.

"Ya feel it, Billyshanks? Ya sweatin' now? Is yer gut all twisted up too? You feel it, Billyshanks. Ya feelin' kind now?"

I'm not. None of it. I'm fiending like a motherfucker. All I want is a goddamn Worm and we are so close my hands are shaking something fierce in anticipation. I'm afraid I won't be able to contain it all if I vent it. So I nod a negative to Billy.

Billy smiles a crooked grin at me as he turns into a gap in the fence of a middle class backyard. Larry Boots and his little crew are waiting on us, the sliding side-door open and Dirty Josh stroking a shotgun as if it were his own dick. Babycakes blows us a kiss and Lila growls.

"Let me the fuck out."

CHAPTER TWENTY-TWO

I OPEN THE ROOF AND CLIMB OUT FIRST.

Lila wants to spring out but I make her hand me the duffle bags full of guns first. Her eyes are full-on shimmering rainbow orbs by the time I allow her to slither out of the tankcar. She hits the ground and drops into a crouch. Her tar black hair falls over her beautiful face obscuring the scowl she is wearing. She springs towards the van before anyone has much time to react.

Far too late, a confused Babycakes mumbles, "Lila?"

Lila lifts the fist at her side, but she opens it up and flattens it. Babycakes stares at Lila's stiff hand. Lila snaps her hand to the side and drives it into Babycakes' throat.

"Holy shit." Larry Boots and I mutter in unison. We chuckle and point at each other as a gagging Babycakes tumbles out of the van into the dirt at Lila's feet.

"Oh, you do remember me? Huh, bitch?"

Lila doesn't give a still choking Babycakes a chance to respond before she kicks the blond in her ample chest with the bottom of her foot. Babycakes crumples backwards, smacking the back of her head on the van as she falls. Lila follows up with a few short but savage kicks to the fallen woman's stomach.

"Damn, okay." Larry Boots says looking at Lila and then to me as if he expects me to stop her.

I shake my head. "Have at it, man. I'd let them work it out."

Larry's wide eyes go back and forth between the women and me. "Hey, ain't you the cat that waxed Charlie Wizard?"

Babycakes catches Lila's foot, spreads it wide and punches her in the crotch from below. Lila crumbles, but does so with a pained look on her face and fists swinging down on Babycakes.

"Yeah, that's me." Killing Charlie Wizard has made me famous on the depraved junkie scene. Yay.

"Well, thank you! That motherless son-of-a-fuck, well, you know, I owes you one."

I don't know how to answer. I nod at him, but my eyes are still on the brawling women. Babycakes has rolled on top of Lila, who is belly-down on the ground and having her throat squeezed shut from behind. Lila's lips turn a shade paler, a thin stream of blood trickles from her left nostril, and her eyes are glowing sweet murder. Still gagging, she throws a wild elbow back and catches Babycakes right between her tits. Lila's sharp elbow thuds against breast plate and Babycakes tumbles off her with a wheezing whimper. Lila pushes up off the ground and kicks both feet backwards like a mule smashing into her adversary's battered torso.

Billy pops his head out of the tankcar, watches Lila put the feet to Babycakes for a minute then hollers at Lila. "What the fook, Billyshanks? Knock that shit off now." Billy starts climbing out of the tankcar but ducks back down when Immunie troops start chattering back and forth on the walkie-talkies.

"Yeah, e-fucking-nough," Dirty Josh growls as he steps towards Lila, rolling his shoulders and flexing muscles that were most likely far more impressive before the whole body-by-Worm he flexes now.

He reaches for Lila and she ducks away and then darts forward too swiftly for him to raise his hands. She drives the edge of her hand into his throat as she had to Babycakes seconds before. I don't think his eyes could bulge any more, but Lila instantly proves me wrong when she follows up with a fist right into his crotch. Dirty Josh grumbles colorful obscenities at Lila through gritted teeth as he crumbles at her feet.

With her attention on Dirty Josh, Lila doesn't see Babycakes roll to her feet wiping bloody drool away from her quivering lips.

The diminutive blond reaches her fists up. She grabs two full handfuls of Lila's straight black hair. Once Babycakes has a firm enough grip she swings all her weight and smashes Lila's head into the side of the armored van. Lila struggles against her smaller attacker, but suffers one more headbutt to the metal van before she catches Babycakes in the face with a wild elbow.

The two battling females both fall down simultaneously and both roll immediately back to their feet to fight on. Billy leaps out of the tankcar holding the walkie-talkie to his ear. He runs to stand in between them acting as peacekeeper. "All yah Billyshanks, better be cool! It is time to go!"

Larry Boots restrains Babycakes, and so I follow his lead and grab Lila by the scruff of her tee-shirt. The women continue hissing and snarling at each other, their shimmering eyes mirroring each other. They thrash violently against our efforts to restrain them, but neither Larry Boots nor I relent. They continue making primal noises at each other until they are just pathetic whelps and whines which hint at a shared painful emotional past for the two. Dirty Josh is on his hands and knees with one hand cupping his smashed delicates.

"I know how they are attackin'!" Billy shouts through a maniacal grin as he kneels in the dirt in the middle of us all. He begins drawing in the dirt with one and raises his sock-puppet hand to explain his excitement to us. "Wuchong, Camsta, and Mafint are each leadin' squads. Mafint from 32nd Street, ov'r 'ere," Billy draws a large sloppy arrow in the dirt on the far side of the rectangle he drew to represent the massive Church of the Dying Star. Then he hastily adds one matching arrow at either end for the other two cyborg warriors. "They expectin' the boys yah waxed," he points at me with the sock-puppet, "ta be hittin' here, at the freight entrance. We'll still hit it, and kill them fooks if they get in the way!'"

He jumps straight up into the air and begins splitting our supply of ill-gotten guns with Larry Boots. Lila and Babycakes have simmered down and now pass looks of shame and hurt back and forth. Dirty Josh is back to his feet, but walking with a noticeable limp. The tattooed dirt-bag is helping Larry carry his loot, whistling at the large cache of weapons Billy tucks back into the tankcar. I stand in the same spot just watching everyone. The feeling this is the last time we will all see each other seems to be the clearest sensation I have experienced sober in weeks. Lila and Babycakes must feel it too because they walk to meet each other and share a long emotional hug just before we load up.

Before he starts the tankcar, Billy turns to us. "Thank yeh both, Billyshanks."

"We getting Worms at the end of this bullshit, Billy?" I make no effort to soften my tone.

"Yeah, Billyshanks, all yeh can carry."

"For me too?" Lila asks, her voice squealing slightly with need.

Yes! Both of yeh!" Billy waves his sock-puppet in the air above him as he starts the tankcar with his other hand.

"I don't want none of the mutant Worms, Billy. I want the normal, smooth glowing Worms. Are you sure the Church has any?"

"They 'ave a monopoly on the Worms...all the Worms in the city are controlled by The Church of The Dying Star. It is the last place yeh can find any."

CHAPTER TWENTY-THREE

MY THOUGHTS ARE A JUMBLED MESS.

Lila holds my hand a little too tightly with her sandpaper paws. Worms are finally on the fucking horizon, and all we have to do is storm an armored compound full of drug-crazed raping murdering zealots. I'll dance with bloody foot-prints through their heathen temple for a god damn Worm. I swear I can feel MOLLY humming in my grip, ready to spray hot death in my quest for Worms. Billy is rotating between sobbing and giggling and speaking nonsense words while looking to the skies. The mood is a tense mix of insanity and desperation which seems to engulf us all.

Billy gets us within just a few blocks of the Church's east wall before he pulls to the side and lets Larry Boots pass him. Larry stares at us as he passes, his dark eyes shimmering neon. Billy eases behind Larry in order to see if any other patrols were around. One block away from the wall we spot one. A cyborg with machine gun arms stands in front of a crowd of men

WORMS IN THE NEEDLE

scattered amongst two more armored cars similar to ours. The monster looks a lot like the cyborg that died in the basement fire, and it waves Larry Boots towards the wall as it yells as the squad surrounding it.

"Rajah," Billy says as he watches the cyborg fall in place behind Larry Boots in the accelerating van. Billy swerves around the crowd of running Immunies and the three other armored cars that pull out in front of him.

Before we all reach the street we hear and feel a series of violent explosions all around us. And with that, so begins the siege of The Church of the Dying Star.

Larry careens the armored van straight for the chain gate and the armed Starries standing right in front of it. The four kimono clad men scream as Larry accelerates towards them, but they don't open fire on Larry until a deacon with a raccoon mask joins them in front of the fence. The Raccoon Deacon raises his MP5 and opens fire at Larry's van, then spots the rest of us as Rajah returns fire from just behind the van. Without warning the two Starries on either side of him, Raccoon Deacon dives out of the way as Larry reaches them and rolls through the four of them and feeble chain fence they protect. Their Worm-eaten insides are pulverized by the speeding machine and spray up over the roof of the van while larger chunks get spat up at us from the van's wheels.

Raccoon Deacon rolls back to his feet with his yellow coveralls splattered with small wet chunks of the other guards. He doesn't even bother with Larry Boots, and instead turns his attention on the approaching Immunies on foot. His MP5 barks to life and the two Immunie troops nearest him fall to the ground with ragged holes drilled through them. Unfortunately for Raccoon Deacon, his fine shooting draws Rajah's murderous attention. The terribly scarred twelve-foot cyborg stomps in Raccoon Deacon's direction yelling in a harsh gravelly voice as he forces Billy to swerve around his angry advance. Lila and I spin around in place and watch Raccoon Deacon's last stand against the furious cyborg through a small slot in the metal armor. It isn't long or pretty, but it leaves a pretty stain on the sidewalk.

Once through the fence the other guards make their selves known. My ears are ringing with the chatter of gunfire as I watch the battle through the slot. The Immunie troops are trying to shoot as they charge, but the Starries waiting just within the wall have much better aim from their semi-protected hiding spots. I watch with wide-eyes as another three troops are torn to shreds with bullets from every direction. Rajah hasn't stopped yelling or firing the massive garrison guns at the ends of his arms and his wild-man tactics quickly avenges his men's deaths in spades.

The Starries are so desperate to slow our advance they throw themselves at Larry's van. He gleefully runs over the kamikazes as he leads us into the side of the massive Church warehouse. As we near the entrance, two deacons- a chubby man in orange coveralls and a panda mask and a skinny man in bright blue coveralls and a tiger mask, appear. Tiger Deacon swings the RPG launcher from his back and takes aim at our tankcar.

"Shit!" Billy howls as he swerves us in front of another armored car which may have been a Ford Mustang.

Sensing his shot lost, Tiger Deacon adjusts his aim to the car behind us. We enter the warehouse on Rajah's huge steel heels but the rush of heat, light and noise directly behind us lets us know the hit was direct. We follow Larry down one more dark turn into an even darker tunnel. After much cursing Billy finds the headlamp switch and dim light floods the darkness to reveal the long corridor-like room we are in. Larry doesn't have time to come to a complete stop and cranks his wheels hard to the side so the van crashes into the wall side-first. Billy pumps the brakes but smashes into the other side of Larry's van. The armor on the side of the van saves those inside, and stops our tankcar hard enough that we all slam forward into Billy's seat and the dash. Two other armored cars pull quickly in behind us, trying like hell to crowd forward. The troops on foot are continuing to be slaughtered by the posted up Starries in spectacularly violent fashion but we have ran out of room to run and lost our battering ram.

Rajah bellows in frustration at the dead end and subsequent pile-up. His harsh gravelly voice crackles through the walkie-talkie. I hear no fear in the squelching cyborg voice, only cold mechanical hate. He calls for backup, and several voices answer. Most I do not recognize, and all have explosions, screams, and gunfire in the back ground. The first voice I do recognize is Mafint's high pitched squeal and he is telling Rajah he had his hands full near the alter room. The second voice I recognize as a voice from the grave. It is Sgt. Stan and he says he is leading a squad this way.

The troops in the last two cars empty out, firing at the Starries attempting to completely box us in. The few remaining foot soldiers dodge bullets as they scamper around the parked cars. Lila and I peel ourselves off of the dash, but Billy shoves us back down.

"Jus' wait for a minute, Billyshanks. Let 'em leave."

We collectively hold our breath and listen to the battle outside of the car. I crawl across the cargo space and stare out the slot in the metal. The doorway is filling up with men and women in neon kimonos, each firing as they creep forward. Without warning the advancing line of Starries I am watching gets torn into wet little ribbons from the massive bullets from some unseen assassin's weapon. The next instant the executioners reveals themselves as Sgt. Stan rolls into view on and right atop his fresh kills with ugly tank treads where his legs used to be. Two 50 caliber repeating guns are mounded on the frame of his tank legs. His face and chest are badly scarred and his left hand has been replaced with a strange looking metal gun barrel of some sort connected to a large gray box fused to his back. He is quickly surrounded by a small squad of gasmask-clad troops armed with an array of high powered artillery.

Atop his kills, Sgt. Stan waves Rajah and his trapped squad out into the wide corridor. The troops abandon their armored vehicles in their rush to safety. None make any attempt to see if we survived the crash, or if we were trapped, they just fell in line, merging cyborg-led squads and continuing inwards of the massive patchwork temple.

We are alone with the fallen from the battle in a silence which seems frenzied after the chatter of gunfire.

In an end to the silence, the windshield of the van swells and crackles as Larry and Babycakes kick at it. It finally comes loose with a shattering poop and falls away still for the most part one shimmering sheet of broken glass. Seconds later, Dirty Josh dives out and over the small steel-covered hood. He falls, lands hard on his back. When he rolls to look in our direction blood trickles thick and steady down his face from a wound in the middle of his forehead.

"Can we get out now, Billy?" I ask already waddling towards the hatch.

"Yah, Billyshanks, and grabs some other goons."

"I got the one I like, Billy, and a knife or two."

"Yah, Billyshanks, yeh'll need some more." Billy answers while grabbing the rest of the bag and waddling past me and out the hatch.

I look to Lila, pale and sweating, trembling with need and want, so sickly beautiful. She has banana-clip heavy rifle in her arms, and a hand gun tucked down the front of her patchwork pants. I'm suddenly so jealous of her cold steel gun barrel I must give her crotch a threatening look because she snaps her fingers there to get my attention.

"You think we're gonna die, baby?" Her voice blurs my soul like a blood smear on a window.

"We are gonna die, everything dies. To dust to dust, our death is our only truth."

"Here? Will we get dusted here and now, I'm saying."

No answer comes to my racing mind, as if every thought I have avoids her question like roadkill in the middle of a highway. I shrug.

"If we want Worms, this is what we have to do to get them." My logic is cold, but she understands the loop my brain is on.

She rubs one slender palm on her forehead as if trying to massage away the throbbing addiction. I feel frustration coming off her in waves, the car is feeling cramped. I waddle after Billy. She grabs my ankle before I can climb out. I lay MOLLY on the roof of the tankcar. Before ducking back inside to face her, I look to see Billy waiting impatiently for Larry Boots and Dirty Josh to help Babycakes out of the crashed and pinned van through the gaping hole where the windshield had been. The feisty blond is scratched and bleeding as well but not near as bad as Dirty Josh, Larry looks like he escaped injury though impact somehow.

Slowly, I drop even with Lila to look her in her shimmering eyes. "Do you want to leave?"

Tears fill her eyes, spill over and drizzle down slender cheeks.

"It's not that, we could die here. Who were you before the Worms?"

"C'mon already, now is not the time to hash this out. I'm a fucking Worm-junkie now. Just like everybody else…"

"Okay, fine. Now you are a Worm-junkie asshole, but what about before? Who is this Charlie Wizard guy every keeps thanking you for killing? "

"Jesus, Lila, Billy is gonna freak out if we don't move our asses and you really want a history lesson?"

"Yes." Her voice sounds firm, yet a little shocked, as if her simple answer will really work.

"Tough shit, toots." I try not to laugh at her, but my best effort is a blood-soaked giggle from biting the inside of my cheek.

She aims her gun at me. The rainbow sheen colors her eyes, and her upper lip twitches like a feminine Scarface ready to shred me.

"If you kill me, you'll never find out the answers to all the mysteries of this Worm-addled killer."

From outside Billy snaps something at us, the others grumble after him in irritated unison.

"We gotta go, baby. I don't know why this is so impor-"

"Because we could die here, baby! Because once we climb out of here either one of us could be shot dead by one of the hundreds of crazy gun-toting psychos running roughshod through this temple! I might never get another chance to hear it!"

"I was a nothing. I drank too much, slept too much, watched too much TV."

"I don't believe you."

"Well, again, tough shit, toots. That's all the truth I got for you right now." The blood from chewing on my inner cheeks is smeared across my teeth when I smile at her.

"God damn it, Billyshanks!" Billy punctuates his impatience by slapping the side of the armored tankcar.

"We gotta go."

She nods and follows me out the hatch.

Billy and the others are standing in a half-circle around the tankcar; bloody, nervous, and fiending. As I grab MOLLY and hop onto the concrete a door behind Dirty Josh bursts open and three Starries dash through, stopping cold when they see us. We make eye contact, rainbow-sheened eyes all of us, and raise our weapons. Dirty Josh ducks and Billy and I fire right where he was standing, peppering the Starries with hot death before any of them get off a shot. Lila and Babycakes take off the same direct the Immunies went, but Billy calls them back with a snarl.

"Oi! This way, Billyshanks!"

The women spin back around so quickly they tangle up and fall to their knees. I reach them, and help them both up while they wince and whimper from their battle wounds. Larry reaches for

Babycakes and she collapses into his arms. Billy reaches into the duffle bag he gave them, retrieves a shotgun, and wedges it in between them. Dirty Josh picks the dead Starries clean of weapons, but finds no Worms. He stands up and smears his blood all over his face, a crimson war-mask. Billy stomps pasts him, kicking the Starry corpses in his path as he disappears through the hidden doorway. I shake my head at Billy's soured attitude, but follow right behind him, a hungry MOLLY in my hands begging for meat to sizzle into and hungry NEED chewing my soul in lieu of Worm-meat.

CHAPTER TWENTY-FOUR

ONCE THROUGH THE DOORWAY WE ARE IN A DARKENED HALLWAY.

It was lit only by the bright fluorescent paint all over the walls. A variety of colors depict all size and rendition of Worms among colorful starbursts. The paint casts no significant light, but defining the wall as it does makes navigation relatively easy in the complete darkness. Billy walks quickly, the gun heavy duffle bag he totes swaying slowly back and forth over his shoulder, and we all struggle to keep up. I shift MOLLY in my arms so I can rest my palm on the wall, and drag it over all the colors as I walk forward.

After a few sudden cuts in the hallway, we dash into a brightly lit room which communally blinds us. Dirty Josh stumbles forward, blinded equally from his flowing blood and the sudden invasive glare from above, knocking us all aside as he charges the blurry shapes he sees in the furious brightness like a drunken rhino. I shield me eyes and attempt to blink the blindness away, even as Dirty Josh begins firing his gun. Babycakes fires her shotgun, but I don't know if she intends to or if panic pulled the trigger for her. It doesn't matter as someone else returns fire on us, but at least I am still too blinded to see where it is coming from.

Without thinking I raise MOLLY and let her sing. Lila fires from right next to me, the clatter of her gun higher-pitched than sweet MOLLY, and I feel the wind from shells whizzing past my face. Within seconds, my vision returns enough for me to see we have wiped out our adversaries, though the others still fire into the blinding light.

"Okay! We got them!" The others cease fire, and commence rubbing their eyes.

I blink away the painful blurriness, and look upon fresh carnage. The first body my aching eyes land on is Dirty Josh's. With her one panicked blast Babycakes managed to nearly cut him in half, and spatter his innards a good fifteen feet away from him. Beyond our fallen comrade lay a half-dozen bullet-riddled Starry carcasses and a dead deacon with an uncomfortable looking crocodile mask; all surrounding a hunched over man in a bright green robe.

The others regain their sight, but don't notice the survivor yet.

"Damn, Babycakes, you done killed the fuck outta Dirty Josh," Larry Boots chides her.

Billy finally notices the wounded bishop and pulls the trigger on his gun. It clicks empty, the hollow metal sound jerking the bishop's head up as if attached by a cord. Billy growls, tosses his empty gun and digs in the duffle over his shoulder for another one.

The bishop watches Billy for a second then turns his wobbly gaze upon each of us in turn. His wide brown eyes are blood-shot under thick brown eyebrows. His nose is wide and prominent, but his curling mustache and blood-soaked beard balance out his face.

Billy finds another weapon, a small semi-automatic with two neon bandanas tied to its beveled barrel, and aims it at the bishop.

"Oh!" the bishop burps to life, acting as if he only now has regained his sight as well. When he stands up straight I see the entire front of his robe is tattered and blood soaked. "Hello strangers, I am Bishop Reade from the Church of the Dying Star. You're here for the Worms, right?"

He doubles back over in obvious pain for a moment, we allow it, and he continues, "Well, they are around here somewhere. But you know what, strangers? The Worms will eat us all! They ate our morals and our science and our gods and our cities and our children and our souls and our-"

I've heard enough, and MOLLY ends his rant and unbalances the symmetry of his face.

Billy smiles at me with Bishop Reade's blood splattered all over his face. He gives me a cheesy thumbs-up and walks over the corpses to look at a plaque on the wall behind the slaughter. I follow him, slipping a little in the pooled blood, and stepping on the Crocodile Deacon's destroyed chest but not falling down. The women follow me, gingerly, careful not to step on the dead. Larry Boots is kneeled down next to Dirty Josh, wiping the blood smeared across his dead friend's face away.

"Man, I known this cat since before the Worms, ya know." Tears stream down his dark cheeks but Larry makes no effort to wipe them away. "We done shared everything, always." I sneak a look at Babycakes and find her unmoved by Larry's tearful farewell. "Damn, bitch, you done killed my best friend."

"I'm sorry, Larry, it was an accident." Babycakes sounds sad, but she wears indifference on her face while she stares at Larry's hitching back.

"Yeah, I know, I was blind as shit too. But, damn, you killed his dirty ass."

I turn away from their exchange to look at the sign on the wall with Billy. It lists a series of rooms (Alter Room, Feasting Hall, Storage Complex, Deacon's Quarters, Bishop's Quarters, General Housing, Pleasure Area, Science Labs, Dirt Fields, and High Priest's Chambers) with each room listed alongside an arrow pointing to either the left or the right. Only the Alter

Room, Pleasure Area, Dirt Fields, Bishop's Quarters and High Priest's Chambers lie to the left, the direction Billy is leaning.

"Billy we are mid-attack, where are we going? Where are the fucking Worms you promised us?" Explosions and gunfire sound all around us, as the Starries and Immunies battle throughout the massive temple around us, so I nearly shout without meaning to.

Billy pokes his sock-puppet hand at the sign, tapping first the Dirt Fields and then the High Priest's Chambers. "Worms 'ere, man I gotta kill 'ere."

"You are here to kill the fucking high priest of The Church of the Dying Star? Holy shit, Billy, he is more protected than the president ever was." I lower my voice but I can't keep the venom I feel over his idea from my tone.

"No!" Babycakes and Lila both shout. They share a look, something old and torn and shining, and then Lila elaborates. "Fuck no, Billy! We are here for Worms! Not suicide!"

"Dirty Josh died for Worms, man!" Larry Boots wails from behind me.

The sounds of battle are drawing ever closer though we haven't moved. Because of the random sharp-cornered hallways and poorly constructed walls which bulge and sink it is difficult to tell which direction the nearest fight is. Billy shouts over the noise, with his sock-puppet hand bobbing in the air while he tells us, "Either way, dis way."

He stomps to the left and we quickly follow after him. The instant Larry Boots passes the sign the wall explodes in a cloud of drywall and dust and the destroyed hallway fills with Immunie troops and Starries battling with swords, spears, axes, and war-hammers. We turn on them, and kill them all before they realize who is shooting them. Another deacon, a hideous Hyena Deacon, turns around just in time to draw his arm back, deadly spear at the ready, before Lila blows out his knee caps. He falls on his spear, and is covered by corpses in the next instant. We flee the scene even as reinforcements from both sides begin crowding in and picking up where the ones we slaughtered had left off.

We reach a high arching doorway, and step onto what looks like a vast construction site smack in the middle of the temple. Half-demolished buildings litter the acres of dirt before our eyes, hunched and dead waiting to fully crumble or be covered over in the thick black dirt. The ground itself is lumpy and swollen, small dunes and little dips of the Worm fertile soil. I squint my blood-shot eyes and see an arm, pale and skeletal and dotted with track marks, poking lazily from a dune and hugging the hillside. Upon closer inspection the landscape is pockmarked with corpses peeking through the Worm-rich soil.

"The fuck, Billy?"

"Mah ol' neighborhood. The Dirt Fields!" Billy waves his arms like a magician revealing his biggest trick, though it fills him with an unholy grief.

"This isn't a dirt field, Billy. This is a mass grave." I hear my own voice as if it is floating on the cemetery breeze.

"It's a mass grave on top of a dead neighborhood, man." Larry Boots corrects me with a whisper.

Lila grabs my arm, her god damn nails biting into the tender flesh they find there, and points the barrel of her gun at a clutter of shovels and buckets about forty yards away from where we are standing. And littered around the split buckets and discarded shovels tiny glowing shapes which the sight of dries my throat and engorges my cock with a rush of excited blood…WORMS.

My legs are moving before I realize it, and I'm tromping over moist black dirt. Six or seven steps in; my left foot sinks ankle-deep into soil. I flail my arms to regain my balance, waving MOLLY in the air with such fervor it almost tips me over. I wiggle the toes on my left foot in a vain attempt to determine if I've lost my flip-flop or not. I don't feel it, only thick oozing sludge. I curl my toes and lift my foot out of the mire. It forms a hollow mound of dirt as it slips free from the earth dripping the pungent gore of the mostly decomposed body I stepped in. The remaining steps in between me and the Worms are slow and cautious.

Lila, Babycakes, and Larry are all following me now, navigating soft spots on tip-toes. It would be comical it I wasn't so focused on the Worms ahead of me. They had the hindsight to drop their guns, so they move with a little more balance than I. Billy watches us from the very edge of the dirt field, but makes no attempt to join us in our trek. No Worms for him then, is all I can say about that.

Three steps, two steps, I reach the Worms. I almost crumble into a weeping ball right here. The small glowing Worms react to me, curling up so the small sharp spikes on their backs stab out defensively. They hiss a sound so tinny and evil my throbbing dick goes flaccid instantly. All of the Worms from this bucket are mutants. The sight of the new Worms rolls my stomach with a nervous fear I thought their simpler cousins had blissfully smashed out of me.

I turn to the next pail choking on this nervous fear as Lila reaches the first bucket and reacts much as I did. The second bucket yields the same findings only worse due to the half-exhumed body the pail rests against. The corpse is green and purple, barely holding a shape remotely human. From the thing's neck to stomach the soft flesh has sunk in and I can see the mutated Worms swimming in the gelatinous decay. The diggers working here had been picking through this corpse-yuck for these nasty spiked Worms. They must have been called into battle when the Immunies attacked, dropped their shovels with glee I'd bet. The others reach me; Lila's eye reflecting the hollowness she feels seeing these new Worms, Larry looks filled with a frenzied panic which makes me glad I'm still cuddling MOLLY, and Babycakes just sobs quietly while holding her need-aching stomach. The walk back is careful and silent.

Billy shakes his head at us as we approach. He holds up his sock-puppet hand and tells us off.

"Yup. New Worms grown up in flesh, not dirt. Old Worms are gone. Grow too slow, need 'em faster, faster, faster. Thems what happens when yeh mess with 'em. Nasty lil' Billyshanks, huh? But, Have at 'em, all yeh Billyshanks!"

"Wait, Billy, Wait." Lila stands in front of Billy with her gun pointed at his belly-button.

I step around Billy, reach over and gently point Lila's gun barrel at the ground, and tell him, "I ain't putting one of them spiked Worms in me. They didn't call to me like the others, they scare me. There has to be the old Worms around here somewhere. I'll follow you to the High Priest's Chambers and help you do what you gotta do, but then, you have to find us some fucking Worms, Billy!"

Billy throws both of his arms around me and pulls me close, crushing MOLLY in between our bodies. He whispers his appreciation into my ear, and I notice his strange shifting accent is gone. Mid-thank you we all hear a loud squealing whistle from deep across the dirt fields. We all turn and face the whistle, Billy still wrapped around me. A faint glow swerves near the distant ceiling then drops into the skeletal remains of an apartment building 400 yards away. A thunderous boom erupts from within the remains, decimating the destroyed structure and those near it in a ball of green flame. The hell-hot green flames lick at the soil boiling the corpses beneath it until they burst in geysers of smoking purple and green rot all around the point of impact.

While we are being terrified and awed by the fallout, a second whistling light drops into the small burnt out remains of a corner gas station closer by 200 yards. We feel the heat from the second blast and I can hear the small popping explosions of the Worms burning as the green flames sizzle and boil their corpse-beds. We stagger back from the encroaching flames, even as the dirt field crowds with armed Starries rushing out to meet the Immunies charging over the flaming graveyard landscape towards us.

We see Rhino Deacon, Hippo Deacon, Ram Deacon and Fox Deacon each leading large squads of Starries clad in brightly colored heavy armor from different angles. Fox Deacon leads his squad to the nearby remains of an apartment building where they take up positions throughout. Hippo Deacon and Ram Deacon each lead a squad on the outside edge of the dirt fields, and Rhino Deacon's squad barrels straight forward to meet the advancing Immunies.

When the Immunies finally come into view, I see Rajah, the squealing Mafint, the newly converted tank-cyborg Sgt. Stan, and a massive cyborg I know as the silent yet deadly Camsta leading a massive horde of Immunies over the dirt fields. All of the cyborgs except for Sgt. Stan have a hard time managing the soft dirt and soupy corpses it covers, so the tank-tred commander meets the Staries first both his mounted guns roaring. The armored Starries run fearlessly into battle, most armed with the double-edged swords and bladed staffs, and their armor deflects all but direct shots from Sgt. Stan's high-powered guns. The Immunie troops were the pillaged military armor they could pillage but it is no match for the Starry weapons close in, and we watch the brightly colored Starries cut the drab-colored foot soldiers to shreds. Fox Deacon's squad plays sniper and picks off the Immunie troopers who make it past Rhino Deacon's commandos.

The Church of the Dying Star looks sure of victory until the third whistling bomb drops on the apartment where Fox Deacon's squad is hiding. The green flames cook the armored Starries where they stand, melding flesh to fluorescent colored metal in seconds. Their dying screams overpower even then constant clatter of Immunie gunfire for a brief instant.

This last explosion is too close for our comfort, and we are pushing our luck enough standing on the edge of the battle field as is, so we back away slowly only to spin around only to be taken by surprise by Ram Deacon and his squad who must have been sneaking up on us. We react quickly for as frayed as our nerves are and open fire as soon as we see them but they charge forward confident in their armor. A Starry manages to grab Babycakes, but she jams her shotgun under his chin and pulls the barrel. Though the buckshot doesn't puncture the metal neck guard, it dents it in enough it slowly strangles the man it is supposed to be protecting.

A Starry in bright yellow armor singles me out, charging and spinning his baton sword in the air. I aim MOLLY at the eye holes in his helmet and squeeze the trigger. My tactic works and MOLLY's bullets puncture the armor's weak point and sink into the Starry skull within the helmet. Billy and Lila both mimic me, and begin aiming for their eyes. Larry Boots wrestles with two staff wielding Starries, swinging his gun like a club until Ram Deacon ends his resistance with a well-aimed bullet to face. The bullet explodes out the back of Larry's brightly colored head and over the battle field behind him.

As one, we turn on Ram Deacon and avenge Larry Boots in quick brutal fashion, picking the dying deacon up off his feet with the force of bullets ripping into him. The air-borne carcass lands at the feet of Bull Deacon, fresh on the battlefield with his combat weary troops. The few remaining members of Ram Deacon's squad try to box us in, but catch bullets to their eyes for their troubles, as we push towards the door. Yet another whistling light glimmers overhead, and we do not want to be around when it lands. The Starries' armor makes them clunky and easy to dart around as long as we watch for the deadly blades they wield at us. Propelled by desperation and fear we maneuver around the Starries and through the door into the lop-sided and uneven hallway as whistling light begins to descend, illuminating everything around us as it nears.

Physically and mentally exhausted, and emotionally drained from the death of her friends, Babycakes falls to her knees just past the threshold to the hallway. Billy, Lila, and I all stop running to look back at her. The light behind her is ever increasing in brightness until Bull Deacon temporarily blocks it out completely as he steps through the doorway to wrap his massive arms around the distraught Babycakes. He hoists her up into the air with so much force I wouldn't be surprised if he broke a number of her fragile ribs. The next instant green flames engulf them, fusing them together as a pitch-black silhouette against the shimmering neon green flames before turning them to a crumbling statue of glowing neon ash. As soon as they dissolve in the flames the doorway and wall around them does the same until it all collapses down, closing us off from the hideous dirt fields forever.

CHAPTER TWENTY-FIVE

WE RUN, AND THE HALLWAY BEHIND US FOLDS IN ON ITSELF AS WE PASS THROUGH IT.

We hear the squealing of bending support beams, and the crashing of corrugated steel walls twisting and tearing under the heat and pressure. We reach a small staircase and all leap all the way down without touching a stair. None of us land gracefully, and instead we end up in a tangled mess of limbs and turquoise jewelry. The staircase clogs with rubble so tight only a gust of fine dust hits our sprawled and helpless forms as it is exhaled from the chaos like a sigh from a dying god. We all lay there for a moment slowly untangling ourselves. Once free, Lila falls back on me, soaking my chest with her rampage of tears. Billy crawls over to the wall and rests against it. He rips his goggles from his face and throws them at the bottle-necked debris jammed into the staircase.

I squeeze Lila against my chest, a numbing sensation radiating throughout my body. I know lying here, bloody and sore from battle and need and covered in the dust of crumbling temple, I will die today. There is nothing left, no benefits to survival, no need worth satisfying to sustain me another day in these dark new days. Lila and Billy feel it too. Billy could have been feeling it when he stumbled upon us earlier. Maybe the others felt it too in the fading high of their last Worm together. They even shared it with me; a bond of sexual frenzy, sweat and cum, I should have known it. My emotions have always been slow to swim to the surface, choosing rather to drown in confusion and coldness. It doesn't surprise me that I'm a step behind everyone else.

I run my slightly trembling hands through Lila's dark smooth hair, silken spider web tickles. I plan my words, the memories and thoughts have been stirring since the first time she asked me about it all, but my voice is still brittle and hoarse.

"I really was a nothing before the Worms, baby. I cooked at a shitty run-down diner for less money an hour than anything you could order off the menu. I worked late shifts because I was always too hung over to work the early ones. I had a wife once, but lost her long before the Worms came. I was sleep-walking through life; baby, blinded bloody by apathy and worn down with dull contentment like the rest of the legions. A scarecrow gutted of individuality and motivation and stuffed full of pop-culture and sloth, hanging like a sinful Jesus scaring cannibalistic crows away from blackened fields."

Lila's tears relent. Billy looks at me with eyes so bloodshot they look like he could weep crimson tears. My eyes are dry and itchy, covered with a layer of temple dust; no tears could form in my parched tear-ducts.

"Charlie Wizard was my brother. And, baby, he was a born hustler, always scamming, always plotting. But when the

Worms came the stakes for everything increased, and his scams became a lot more dangerous. When the Worms came, Charlie emptied the pot, coke, DMT, and MDMA from his supply closet and had Tupperware tubs full of graveyard dirt in their place. He was an Immunie, but not hard-wired for Wormer destruction like the rest, no Charlie Wizard wanted everything the Worms could give him except the high. So he dealt with the diggers like Billy, and the street slingers like Larry Boots, and he dealt with the Church of the Dying Star. And since he was an Immunie he was selling info to the cyborgs just to make sure he had his fingers in every pot he could."

"We always went straight to the diggers, baby. Nobody was selling them just out of their house." Lila makes the point timidly, afraid I'll stop telling my story, but I surprise her by continuing.

"That's because Charlie ended up getting most of them killed. See, Charlie could make anyone feel like his best friend in the whole world, which only made it that much harder to deal with when you find out he has fucked you over. Charlie would buy from the diggers, sell them to the Church with a healthy mark-up and then offer to take a small percentage off in trade for the supply of sickly Worms he would take from them and deliver to the street dealers.

When the street dealers complained, he'd turn them over to the Immunie troops; who would then torture them into giving up their diggers when Charlie had been the one acting as the go between. With no answers to give scores of innocent people across town were senselessly tortured to death and Charlie's pockets just kept getting fatter. Those that survived, went and found their own damn diggers, cutting Charlie out-like he deserved, but most were too paranoid to sell out of their homes so they ended up working security for the diggers instead. So when Charlie starts coming around, all jazz-tongued and slick, all these street dealers turned grave guards got pretty pissed off. Sensing his trade with the diggers in ruins, Charlie told the High Priest of the Church of the Dying Star, he who controls the graveyard controls the Worms."

Across from us Billy chimes in, "And when yeh tell a Worm-chewed psychopath somethin' like that, they go to great lengths ta see it become reality. Like killing entire families- just like the one I used ta 'ave, in order ta 'ave graves in their dirt field."

Billy's quiet revelation steals the air from the room, and threatens to unravel the delicate strings of gossamer memory I'm struggling to grasp as is. I want to tell Billy how sorry I am for his loss, but stopping now while crash my train of thought.

"Yup. The Starries started raiding the cemeteries, and killing or capturing the diggers. Charlie was driving Church to control all the Worm trade in the city and crushing over anyone who got in his way. I lost a lot of friends in those days, and saw the hopelessness on the horizon. You couldn't just walk up and score a few Worms from the temple, you had to join the Church of the Dying Star...and we've seen how that pans out. Charlie showed up one night, trying to sell me a batch of Worms 'fresh from the dirt fields'. I knew they weren't because Lazy Sal and his boys got sliced up that morning, and their six plots over taken by Starries. He was going to make money off of me, his broke-ass, strung-out brother…I kinda' snapped. I beat him until only his feet twitched, and then I dragged him outside and hung him from the cemetery gate by Lazy Sal's stolen plots."

Lila eases off my chest and kisses me on the forehead with her cold pale lips. "Thank you, baby," she whispers, content in our trust on the cusp of our destruction.

Billy nods, "We all owe yeh for 'at, Billyshanks."

I force at smile at him and struggle to my feet. My body crackles and pops, strains and aches. I find MOLLY at my feet and pick her up. Her clip is empty, and Billy passes me the last one from the duffle. He retrieves two handguns, and gives both to Lila as she lost her machine gun in the hallway during our escape. The only gun left is the short barreled mini-machine gun Billy totes. He unties the bandanas from the barrel and rests them across each other at the base of the rubble-blocked staircase, a neon memorial for our friends.

"Jus' up the hall." Billy wobbles off to his destiny and Lila and I embrace and limp behind him.

CHAPTER TWENTY-SIX

THE DOOR TO THE HIGH PRIEST'S CHAMBERS IS AS ORNATE AS I EXPECT.

It's a rich deep red cherry wood with hand-carved Worms slithering along its length. We stand right outside of it and double check our weapons. I fully expect to feel a stoic malevolence from the room, but in the wake of the sounds of battle, the silence consumes my senses and renders my thoughts to a high whirling buzz, too mechanical to comprehend. MOLLY's weight in my hands anchors me to reality, and to the cold finality of it all.

"Thank you, Billyshanks, for this." Billy tells us without turning his teary eyes on us. His blue hair, which was spiked inches off his head at the beginning of our adventure, is now plastered to the sides of his face with sweat and blood. His sock-puppet hand has lost almost all of its googly-eyes and is stained a bright fresh-blood crimson. But he is smiling weakly.

"This is what friends are for, Billy." I answer for Lila and me.

He nods and reaches for the bronze door handle with his sock-puppet hand. He tugs it open and I watch absent-mindedly as yet another toy eye is scraped off of Billy's sock-puppet to clatter across the concrete floor. The heavy door scrapes across the floor, pulverizing the little plastic eye Billy just unknowingly shed. Billy takes a deep ragged breath and leads us into the room.

The walls of the room are neon colored curtains swaying in a breeze I don't feel on my skin. The massive neon tapestries roll and wave into each other, giving me the intense impression of the walls sucking in breath and swallowing it down into the bowels of this cursed temple. So this is the room we are dying in. Neon streamers hang from a rust-eaten chandelier overhead, reaching long slender fingers down to caress the wide shoulders of a high-backed chair in the center of the room. A man with a long thick black beard, but no mustache, and a bright crimson robe sits in the chair staring silently at us. His muscled arms are folded across a barrel chest and steel-toed work-boots poke out from under the hem of his crimson robe.

"Where is High Priest Jones?" Billy's voice is firm, yet quiet, barely above a whisper. His gun is aimed at the bearded man's chest, but the big man seems unfazed by the unspoken threat.

"He is around here somewhere, I am Cardinal Ray. Can I help you with something?" His voice is unnervingly calm and his eyes never leave Billy when he speaks. The corners of his lips curl up in the slightest smile, and I know he knows more than he is letting on.

I have MOLLY pressed to my shoulder and I am staring down her barrel at Cardinal Ray but the swaying walls distort my vision almost to the point of making me ill. Somehow, I think the son of a bitch knows that too, so I lower my gun to rest my eyes from the incessant slight movement all around me. Lila has both her guns on Cardinal Ray as well, but I see her forearm muscles flexing as if they cannot support the weight of the weapons. Even with all of us having him dead-to-rights, Cardinal Ray is still in firm control.

"Yeah," Cardinal Ray stretches, then, stands while speaking. "I thought maybe you were just here for Worms until I saw you all on the dirt field. That got pretty ugly, pretty fast, huh?"

We all nod back at him in a strange absentminded unison.

"Well, you see, I've been watching you all since you crashed through the gate by the warehouse. Figured you'd get what ya came for and be gone."

"Maybe we've seen the light and want to join up." My sarcasm must be a defense mechanism. It doesn't impress Cardinal Ray much.

Cardinal Ray stands slowly from his chair, stretches his arms into the mass of streamers hanging down on him until we hear an audible hollow pop from in between his shoulders, and walks nonchalantly across the room to a gently waving pink curtain. "Usually people who find the faith come right to the front door, and don't kill as many of us as possible."

He grabs the edge of the silken sheet with one meaty paw and gently tugs it aside, revealing a massive wall of video monitors. Over half the monitors are static, and a few completely black, but others still show rooms and corridors throughout the temple in astounding clarity. He has been sitting here watching the attack the entire time. And now, his reward must be the smug-ass grin he wears. The grin, the room, the feeling of panic grinding my guts into a nervous mush, it is all making me dizzy. The world takes on a red tint and I feel numbness tingling in my fingers and toes.

Before I can pass out, the bright orange curtain behind us slides silently to the side and the bishops, including the ones from the park, step into my peripheral vision. I spin on one I've seen one in a purple robe and Bishop Quinto in his pink robe but one grabs MOLLY's barrel at the same time the other tackles me low and hard. Bishop Denton wraps his arms around Billy and jerks him off his feet so hard and fast, Billy drops his gun to his feet. Billy and Cardinal Ray never break eye contact.

Lila reacts even quicker than I, and not only spins on the two behind her but fires off a few rapid rounds in Bishop Waldrop's wide round belly. Her bullets punch a big enough hole the bishop in the blood-splattered yellow robe drops to his knees with both his hands struggling to hold his insides in. A bishop in a bright blue robe chops one hand down across the barrels of her weapons and then issues her a wicked backhand. As she stumbles backwards from the blow the bishop snatches both her guns from her hands in a lightening quick motion.

"Excellent, Bishop Webber!" Cardinal Ray claps his hands and Bishop Webber smiles a crooked goofy grin and tosses both guns on either side of Lila's head for Cardinal Ray to pluck out of the air.

"Bishop Webber?" I ask from the ground with Bishop Quinto's fist tucked under my chin so my voice is strained.

The smug mother fucker spins around to face me with his ridiculous grin. He laughs at me at steps forward a few steps before bending over to blow a raspberry in my face. I kick him in his kneecap as hard as I can from my sprawled position. The force of my kick forces his knee back so hard and fast his weak junkie shin bone snaps. As Bishop Webber is howling while collapsing at my feet, Bishop Quinto's fist comes dislodged and I have enough space to take a deep breath and scissor my legs around Bishop Webber's screaming head. Bishop Quinto abandons the fist in throat tactic and instead pokes his filthy fingers into my eyes, but not before I flex my legs with everything I have and silence Bishop Webber with a series of muffled cracks.

"Son of a bitch," Cardinal Ray huffs.

Lila turns on him, intent on getting her guns back. He simply raises the one in his right hand and shoots her in the head. The bullet doesn't even explode out the back like I expect, she just chokes on what would have been her last words and falls onto the floor between Billy and me.

And like that she is gone. I am truly alone in this dead Worm-eaten world, and ready for death's embrace. The hollow inside me begins to frost over; with the warmth she filled me with dissipating. I fight against the two bishops restraining me and Cardinal Ray puts a bullet in my shoulder. Bishop Quinto takes the opportunity to smash MOLLY's butt into my face a half-dozen times.

The blood dripping in a steady stream off my face and creeping down my throat to my stomach and lungs tells me my nose is broken. The way my vision has gone a strange slow-motion blurry where focus comes in fractals, and which varies between over dim or painfully bright convinces me I have at least one skull fracture from MOLLY's hardened end. Yet the tears cutting paths through my blood smeared face are born from the pain in my heart.

Still, there is no rest for a villain's soliloquy, and Cardinal Ray's irritatingly calm voice returns in the dying echo of gunfire. "Now, see, I didn't want that to happen. I hope you two can be cool." He looks between Billy and I; I am unable to focus on him through the splinters of light dividing my vision but Billy spits a wad of bloody phlegm at him. "Terrible attitudes, brothers. Now is a time of celebration and mirth! The enemy has been turned back! We may rejoice in the mercy of the Dying Star has cast upon our wretched souls!"

His voice is no longer calm by the end of his statement but booming and echoing in the curtained chamber. My vision clears as his timbre raises until his baritone issues a healing vibration. He stomps across the room, waving his arms to enunciate his words, until he is standing in front of a yellow curtain. He tugs the bright cloth to the side to show a line of shelves crowded with decapitated human heads.

"You guys know these two, right?" Cardinal Ray cradles Rajah's head in the crook of one arm and Sgt. Stan's in the crook of his other. Billy fights against Bishop Denton, but with me only half-conscious the bishop in the purple robe leaves me and helps restrain him. I look to the shelf and see Mafint's scarred face frozen in a scream; Sgt. Sluka's bloodied head next to his gas mask, and several other heads I do not recognize. Cardinal Ray puts each head carefully back, and then leans down to wipe his hands on Bishop Webber's robe as his corpse is the closest.

"But they ain't even the prize, boys."

On cue Goat Deacon, in a blackened jumpsuit, and Monkey Deacon, in a blood-splattered butcher's apron, appear and tug aside the bright purple curtain next to Billy. Behind the curtain is a set of wide heavy metal doors, which the deacons open with twin squeals of metal on concrete. Horse Deacon, Cobra Deacon, Lion Deacon, and Hog Deacon wheel in the scraps of the largest cyborg I have ever seen on a long flat metal cart. The pale, scarred form of a man curls and flops within the folds and shards of metal like a human Worm ready for injection.

"Kytrn!" Billy's surprise releases his gasping word before he can stop himself.

Cardinal Ray claps his hands and points at Billy. "That's right! The one and only Kytrn!" The cardinal hisses the name the way people used to say 'Nazi' before the Worms. "The great cyborg leader of the Immunie Resistance! On a slab in the middle of our temple! How about that, boys?"

The bishops and deacons whoop and holler but they all sound pushed to the point of exhaustion.

"Some fancy weaponry in play here fellas." Cardinal Ray lifts one of the cyborg's massive cannon arms. "Now, let's strip that slab of human out of this mess and pillage what we can, boys!" Like ants on a carcass the deacons are on Kytrn with handsaws, knives, and one power-saw wielded by Monkey Deacon. Kytrn bellows and howls as the deacons saw away the bone just above where it has been melded with steel, yank out wires stuck in motherboards embedded under his skin, carve away stubborn flesh growing over his robotic implants, and yank hissing tubes and hoses from his body.

Billy groans, a sound helpless and distraught, and looks at the floor below him, but I keep my fractured vision on Cardinal Ray who walks across to the last neon sheet to be pulled aside, the bright green one. "You see, brother," the cardinal explains to us, "the man-machine you know as Kytrn is actually a power-mad child whose real name is Kevin…Kevin Jones."

Billy makes a confused gagging sound and all the Starries in the room drop to their knees as Cardinal Ray slides the green curtain to the side. Behind the curtain sits a man in a brilliant white and red robe. I force my eyes to focus better and I realize the robe is white and the brilliant red is this man's own blood. His face is crisscrossed in bright red gouges, and where his left eye once was is a sinew filled crater circled by a blackened crust dripping pulpy gore down his cheek. He waves one hand at the men gathered in his office, revealing the two jagged stumps gushing blood all down his arm where his pointer and birdie finger used to be and splattering the small closet he is in with excitedly flung blood.

"Oh, look," Cardinal Ray taunts Billy, "I found High Priest Jones."

The Starries in the room laugh in forced unison, the laughter muffled by deacon mask sounding even less sincere. I sense the change in Billy's mood, he is re-invigorated with sight of High Priest Jones, knowing he still has a chance at the revenge he seeks but he hides it well enough. I see his eyes dart from the insane High Priest Jones to the deacon in the purple robe holding tight to MOLLY next to him and Bishop Denton.

"Our dear father has asked to see his son again, and you two are lucky enough to witness one of the greatest moments of peace for these dark new days. Of course, our spiritual leader cannot gaze upon his son as a monstrosity of steel and flesh, so dear Kevin must deal with some pain in his repentance. Get 'em out, boys. Let him crawl over to his daddy."

Goat Deacon and Monkey Deacon grab the mutilated Kytrn from his cyborg skeleton and drop him onto the cold tile floor. The pale naked man flops as if the sensation of cold tile sends electrical shocks through his body. The deacons have severed his legs just below the knees and his arms just below the elbows. Kytrn's wounds have been rudely cauterized so they don't bleed, but the dozens of gaping holes all over his body where wires and hoses were once affixed drizzle and drip blood and thick diesel-reeking oil all over the floor. Despite the lack of hands and feet, Kytrn flops over onto his badly scarred stomach and begins a slow agonizing crawl towards his high priest father.

As the amputated man crawls through growing puddles of his own blood/oil mix Cardinal Ray reaches in and straightens High Priest Jones's tall neon hat, and picks away the largest chunks of eye pulp he can find on the his cheek. Even with my strange visual effects I can see the sad little smile the cardinal wears while performing his grizzly task.

Billy must notice as well because he asks, "What 'appened ta 'im?"

Cardinal Ray dabs at the deep fresh scratches across High Priest Jones's face and makes no effort to hide his sadness. "Well, after some terrible advice from a long-since vanished-associate, our noble leader ingested some Worms I can only describe as unstable. They had immediate adverse mental effects on High Priest Jones, effects we haven't been able to reverse."

"Was 'at 'fore or after 'e ordered the digger's families killed?" Billy snarls so viciously Bishop Denton tightens his grasp just to be safe.

"No telling." Cardinal Ray admits. "But I can tell you if any of them would have accepted our fair offers it would have never had to escalate like it did. But! None of that matters now, does it? This family gets to be together and we get a chance for peace to rise from the ashes, you self-centered prick! The man has clawed out his own eye and chewed off his own fingers and toes for Worm's sake! If your family got killed by the Church of the Dying Star then they are Worm-chow now, and you will be soon too. So while you still have the time, focus on the positive!"

Billy fights against Bishop Denton's iron grasp until the purple robed deacon smashes MOLLY's butt to his cheek, opening a deep ugly gash. I thrash against Bishop Quinto, weaker than I truly am, and during the struggle I feel the tanto I salvaged from the park tucked in the front of my pants. I will have a last stand after all. When Billy's head snaps to the side, Billy sees me, and we make eye contact. Without using words, Billy tells me he is sorry for the way everything is about to end, but glad I came along. I hope my eyes relay the same to him.

While Billy and I have our final farewell, Kytrn's pitiful blood and oil slick form flop/crawls to his father's giddily kicking feet. Cardinal Ray smiles down at the high priest's son tapping at his father's leg with the nub of charred bone poking from his stump.

Cardinal Ray rests his hand on the high priest's shoulder and speaks in a high bubbly voice like addressing a child, "Look, Jonesy, Kevin came home to be with you."

High Priest Jones claps his hands together like an amused idiot child at mention of the name. When he does I notice his other hand, while not bleeding, is missing two fingers as well so his clumsy claps are a hollow flapping sound. Cardinal Ray reaches down and grabs Kevin/Kytrn under his armpits and picks him up off the floor. He hands the wiggling amputee in his father's arms and stands away to soak in the happy glow of reunited family. All the bishops and deacons sob and smile, some even clapping, as mutilated father and son share an embrace soaked in blood and oil.

Billy has other plans, and he quickly puts them into action. He throws his head back, smashing the back of his cranium into Bishop Denton's wide smiling face, destroying teeth and perfect nose, as well as loosening the death grip on his chest. Just to be sure he has disabled Bishop Denton; Billy kicks one heel back, burying it in the bishop's robe covered crotch. Billy moves so fast the deacon in purple is caught off guard, never seeing his swinging fist before it crashes into the side of his head. As the unknown bishop falls to the ground Billy yanks MOLLY out of his hands, and spins on the high priest and son.

I take the opportunity to roll hard to the side pitching Bishop Quinto off me and into the wall. I reach my hand to the tonto and roll to my feet slashing wildly. The knife drags across Bishop Quinto's throat with more luck than skill as he struggles to knock me back down. His pink robe is instantly soaked in the blood gushing from his gaping wound, and his pale hands weak as they slap at me. I crawl away from the dying bishop as Billy opens fire.

My eyes snap to the small closet High Priest Jones and Kevin are crowded into just in time to watch bullets explode their heads and chest cavities. Everyone is screaming, Billy is the loudest of all, but Billy just holds the trigger down and lets it spray the father and son in a hot shower of personal revenge. Cardinal Ray releases a bellow of rage tinted sorrow, and stomps right across the small room to the cart holding Kytrn's cyborg carcass. He lifts the massive arm cannon and stuffs his fist deep into it. He aims it at Billy, who turns and looks momentarily before returning to his murderous task with a smirk. Still bellowing, Cardinal Ray fires the massive cyborg weapon, sending half-dozen fist-sized balls of hooks and barbs directly at Billy. Three out of six balls hit Billy just above the waist, where Billy is literally torn in half from the impact. One of the other three balls smashes into Billy's face, ripping flesh from bone and leaving his face a pulpy smear. Another hits the purple bishop in the top of his head as he struggles to his feet. His skull is turned to mush and he falls right back down in the same position he had been in. The last deadly ball smashes into the wall of video monitors, showering us all with shards of screen and spat electric sparks.

The moment of chaos freezes for me. Sparks fall all around me in a sizzling slow-motion firestorm, tiny shards of glass slashing at my back and arms. Cardinal Ray is still bellowing and trying to fire the massive weapon at Billy's destroyed corpse again. Several deacons are running into the small closet but there is no saving the high priest or his prodigal son. I can leave, run for my freedom, but now I have my own throbbing need for revenge.

I run across the room low, slashing at the lower legs of the distracted deacon's nearest me- dropping Horse Deacon and Cobras Deacon and ensuring they'll never walk the same again, and diving-knife first at Cardinal Ray. The tanto sinks into his belly with a wet whisper, but I don't manage to knock him off his feet. He laughs, a sound similar to his agonized bellowing, and stares down at the knife plunged into his stomach.

I feel a hot biting sting in my arm, and then a slick unwrapping sensation as my muscle pulls away from bone. Then the same biting sizzling stabs in my side, chest, and neck. The world is tinting red again, and I'm covered in blood. My muscles seize in shock and I flop more than fall to the floor. On my way down I see Goat Deacon pointing my traitorous MOLLY at me as he drains her of her last few bullets. The floor is cold, and slick with blood and oil. I feel my fingers twitching and the damaged nerves around my wounds exploding in pained starburst sensations. I wait for the blackness to take me but it doesn't, I just lay here, wheezing blood and listening to my bullet-clipped lung hiss away my precious last breaths.

CHAPTER TWENTY-SEVEN

IN THE SILENCE OF OUR LAST STAND, I HEAR PEOPLE COUGHING, WHEEZING AND WEEPING ALL AROUND ME.

I can't move and feel my body deflating within itself. When the survivors speak I can't understand them through my wet muffled hearing. Within minutes they are putting all of us in a massive wheel barrel, handled by Goat Deacon and Monkey Deacon, and rolling us out of the high priest's chambers.

As we roll down a darkened hallway, I am able to turn my head enough to come face to face with Lila. I stare into her dead eyes, searching for that glimmer of life you always take for granted. She has no tears frozen in her, only a thin trickle of blood drizzling from the bullet hole in her forehead and down between her eyes. If I could move my arms I would caress her cold cheek one last time.

"So how was the park?" Monkey Deacon asks his partner.

"Good, it'll make a great new dirt field, especially after the cluster fuck here." Goat Deacon has a slight accent but I can't trace it with my unraveling mind.

Monkey Deacon chuckles under his mask, a desperate mocking sound, "Yeah, it got pretty wild pretty fast. We had an idea they were coming, we just got the defenses up a little late. Took some heavy losses, but opens up the chances for promotion. Am I right, man?"

"Yeah, after Cardinal Ray finally becomes High Priest, you and I will be Bishops. We'll get to pick the next round of deacons."

Monkey Deacon drops his end of the wheel barrel suddenly. He shouts, "And we run the new breeding program!"

"Fringe benefits they call that. Pick that back up."

With a huff we get moving again, and are soon pulling into a room thick with smoke, ash and dust. The deacons choke on the rancid air ripe with death and scorched earth, but I can't breathe in enough to.

"Look, this guy has on a sock-puppet, a filthy sock-puppet. Should I take it?" Monkey Deacon pokes at Billy's lifeless hand.

"I'm taking it for Martha; she'll use it to carry her kit." Goat Deacon answers as he reaches in and tugs it off in one rude jerk. Billy's fist flops open with the departure of the ever-present puppet. A locket rolls from his palm to rest on his fingertips. Three faces stare back at me, I almost don't recognize Billy-save for his crooked grin- and I've never seen the woman or little girl before. I close my eyes, but the burning doesn't stop. I reopen them again and stare into Lila's still eyes when they start talking again.

"So why are we dumping them here if you guys got the park dirt field started?" Monkey Deacon asks as he reaches in and tugs at Lila's corpse. Before Goat Deacon can answer, Lila is jerked out of my view, and dropped into a waiting shallow pit.

"This is still going to be a working dirt field. We will rebuild the temple, and work the new dirt field. We will control more Worms than any other branch of the Church of the Dying Star."

"I don't like the new Worms." Monkey Deacon mumbles his confession.

"Yeah, I don't like your blasphemy." Goat Deacon's tone sends a weak chill through my dying body.

"I'm sorry, maybe I just haven't had enough...I'll jack up as soon as we get these bags planted.

"Yeah, we'll go celebrate. Grab that guy's torso, I already got his legs."

They grab me next and jerk and hurl me on top of the others. I blink and wince, and they realize with a shared shock I'm still alive.

"Tough bastard we got here." Goat Deacon says as he pulls a jar from the depths of his blackened coveralls. "Shoulda' died when I killed you, man."

He holds the jar over my bubbling chest wound, and wiggles it until a fat spike-cover Worm slips out and lands right next to it. Goat Deacon whistles a funeral march as he pokes the spiked creature into my gaping wound. Once buried in my ruined flesh the Worm burrows on its own, with what feels like acidic drool.

Convulsing now. Tasting colors-acid poison, feeling colors grinding, rending. Exploding rebirth. Worms feast on flesh and soul, fat with sin. So smooth, so bright.

Hollow, hollow, merciful hollow, darkness, merciful darkness.

...END

If man makes himself a worm he must not complain when he is trodden on. -Immanuel Kant

–ABOUT THE AUTHOR–

When Not under court-ordered chemical restraints, Jonathan Moon writes beautifully brutal horror such as STORIES TO POKE YOUR EYES OUT TO and HEINOUS. He is the co-author of THE APOCALYPSE AND SATAN'S GLORY HOLE with Timothy W. Long. He is an editor for CHRIST-BAIT REHABILITATION CENTER, the hardcore horror division of Dynatox Ministries. His turn-ons include barbed wire, hatchets, and bright neon colors. You can find him on Facebook or at
http://www.mrmoonblogs.blogspot.com

HERE'S A LITTLE BITTY-BIT ABOUT THE HOUSE

Where rules no longer apply. Where profane things occur. What hellions read. So treat your dark self to our insane horror and edgy thrillers. The brutal bible tales. Explore our dark suspense and depraved monsters. Places far off the reservation. The strangest and most entertaining stories anywhere . Go to morbidbooks. Where everything bleeds. All morbidbooks titles are available in paperback and kindle-style e-books at amazon.com, createspace.com and barns&noble.com and discerning serial killers near you.

ALSO AVAILABLE FROM MorbidbookS IN PRINT & KINDLE:

(click on any image in this book for hyperlink)

"IF YOU KNOW WHAT KINBAKU, POST-IMPRESSIONISM, and brilliant green eyes have in common, then you are probably a fan of Alex S. Johnson! Congrats! But if you don't know, allow me to open the door, guide you inside, and introduce you to a little Wicked Candy. This is a sweet designed for the discerning Bizzarro fan's tastes, and I promise, you will not be disappointed!"
--Mimi Williams, author of Beautiful Monster

"A short collection that both traverses the genre lines and melds them together into one masterpiece. Jam packed with horror, laughs, pop culture history and more, this one is a must have for lovers of the macabre, the bizarre and the hilarious."
--Jeff O'Brien, author of Bigboobenstein

IN GARRETT COOK'S MURDERLAND serial killers are idolized by society. Their deeds are followed obsessively by television pundits and the adoring public. A subculture has grown up around this phenomenon, called "Reap." Laws are created to allow this activity to flourish, including designated "safe zones' where killers can practice their trade without fear of persecution. Fans of the top rated serial killers celebrate each new kill on social media and television. Programs glorify their deeds.

The culture of Murderland is violent and mirrors our own violent society and its decadent obsessions; but Murderland isn't about how violent the world has become. It's about the pervasive nature of media and how it corrupts. It corrupts absolutely.

At the heart of Murderland is Jeremy Jenkins. Jeremy doesn't like what he sees and he's just enough insane to believe he can do something about it, that he can change the world. His methods are extreme- to outdo the serial killers, he'll kill THEM, turn their own twisted reality back on themselves. It's a hopeless task, impossible, Herculean; but it's Jeremy's fate to see it through to the end.

The three sections of Murderland comprise a true Homeric epic. In the first section we are shown the terrible world Jeremy lives in, the world that if we look at it honestly, is really our own world. We meet all the principal characters, the serial killers, the pundits, the pawns, and Jeremy's beloved Cass. In the second section Jeremy goes on a bit of a spiritual quest and comes to understand his true purpose. In the final section the flames are ignited and all hell breaks loose. Jeremy, like a great epic hero must journey to the underworld and be reborn in order to triumph.

BORN WHOLE FROM THE RECTUM of a dying patient, Morbid silently stalks the hospital's hallways, heinously dispatching the most helpless of patients and in the most painfully repulsive of manners. In the meantime, in order to pay for his family and home that includes his ghost step-father Sammy and his pet aborted fetus Chip, Westphal has to ingest mounds of dangerous narcotics to get through his night shifts. Barely hanging on to his Care Tech gig by his fingernails, the last thing Westphal needs is to be accused of Morbid's evil deeds. You, on the other hand, simply want to find some solace. Terminally ill from a virulent infection, and dependent on Life Support, all You beg for a peaceful and dignified demise. Shirk has other plans for You. The ancient drug-snuffling demon makes You relive all of your deadly and venial sins as he tortures You. Night after night. Until eternal Damnation begins. Yet again …

IT LOOKS LIKE CAROLYN AND MARK ARE IN DEEP, DEEP SHIT...

Mark and Carolyn live in an alternate 1989 where Ronald Reagan is on his fourth presidential term. The USA has a rigid, long-standing caste system and abortions were never made legal. Being homeless is a crime that is punishable by imprisonment in an internment camp the inmates call Tent City. Most of Mark's ER patients are inmates at this camp and are victims of a new disease these illegals call the Transient Flu. This deadly and rapidly spreading disease mutates with each new host, collecting information, changing code. The disease evolves lightning quick, spreading like pond ripples and infecting everyone. No one is safe. Mark and Carolyn dig too deep and uncover the brutal truth: Transient Flu was purposely made and is one hundred percent fatal. Carolyn's employer, Hudson-Smythe Pharmaceuticals, discovers the chain of evidence. It traces the pharmacide back to Hudson-

Smythe and the crime of the century. Cost is no object and deadly force is authorized. Yes. Carolyn and Mark are in deep, deep shit.

IMMANUEL THE CHRIST HAS SOME NERVE. Jonah has already lost everyone he loves to Pilate the vampire and his Harbor drug violence. Jonah now trudges through his days staying as high on Plata as possible. He just wants to be left alone while he waits for his turn to die. The Christ has other plans for him. She sends Her messenger, Pedro, to assign Jonah the very dangerous task of ordering the Herod to dismantle the Harbor's Plata trade. Jonah decides to run. But you can't run from God forever. As Jonah learns the hard way when the 'Edmund Fitzgerald' founders and goes down in rough seas, with the reluctant prophet on board. Job is Satan's Chosen One and he doesn't take kindly to orders from some upstart prophet. Rather than acquiescing, Job thinks caving Jonah's head in with a tire iron is the best bet. Jonah finds himself out of the frying pan, but firmly fixed in the fire. Then the Lord Herself starts dispatching Job's children. One at a time, until the Herod of The Harbor finally obeys.

SHORT STORIES OF DARKNESS AND DISMAY, snorting souls, Satan and the New Christ make a bet; Pontious Pilate is re-born a vampire, evil ghosts and wicked demons. Dark shit from The Most Depraved Writer in Print. Rage creates a dismal post-industrial future, a look at man defiled and in decline. Evil has arrived. Dominion has been taken by those who walk as the damned, demons, halflings, products of debauched rampages and sins against nature. Sex, drugs, and broken souls are the only things of value. Life is more like a disease, and the only salvation is the right amount of Plata to numb the conscience and, if one is lucky, to bring on a cleverly disguised demise. Through the sheer shock of his presentation, Rage forces readers to consider the alternatives, to look at the garbage in the streets, to see what is swept into the gutters at night right before all decent people awake to see another cleaned up version of the day.

LINES TELL TALES THAT WITHOUT THE RIGHT EXPOSURE live completely disguised within crevices that no amount of washing can remove. Though we yearn to have them clean – enough. Spend hundreds of dollars on this or that to wash ... them ... clean. But some stains never come out, no matter how much we scrub, steam, or sterilize. And what becomes of the hands that are soaked in generations of sins committed by their owners, perpetual motion of offenses against their fellow man time and time again? Isn't there something that we've all done that we just can't seem to cleanse ourselves from? And what if you were Pilate? Steven Rage's "Pilate: A Brutal Bible Tale" explores the depths of sin, the way it stains our lives, and graphically illustrates the things we fear most.

"I'M FEELING DOWN AND DIRTY, FEELING KIND OF MEAN, so I give those fans my middle finger. Those poor bastards go nuts. My team looks at me in awe. My coach frowns and the opposing one begins to furiously scratch out new plays. The Warface is feeling her oats tonight and they all know they're in for a deep snag. I see our opponents and I almost feel sorry for the poor bastards. Their fans can't help them. Their coach can't help them. I'm going to run them off their own track in front of their own fans and there is not one thing they can do about it. I see my counterpart positioning herself on the outside line. I've got my eye on her and I've got her number. She is going nowhere. I'm going to body check her narrow ass off the track and into the third row. I hear the second whistle sound. The jammers are starting to move behind us as I veer toward her. I lower my right shoulder. She sees me at the last second. I smile as her eyes open wide. I get speed, lean in deep and hit her. Silly rabbit, no one gets past the Warface. Not tonight they don't."